S. Cunliffe

"THE PURPLE ORCHID"

Hello, this is my first book and I hope you enjoy reading it. I really want to know what you think of it. If you have picked this book up at a charity shop you may have paid the shop for the book but I do not make any money from the sale. I just want feedback on my writing. Please let me know what you think by writing to me at readers@readscunliffe.com, or go to Amazon.co.uk and leave a brief review that tells me if you enjoyed the book and if you would like to read more stories like the ones in my book. With warmest wishes,

S.Cunliffe

"THE PURPLE ORCHID"

A NOVEL BY S. CUNLIFFE

S. Cunliffe Press

ISBN: 9798320135557

Chapter 1 –

The Purple Orchid

August 2022

In August 2022, as the USA regained a sense of normalcy post-pandemic, the weather turned exceptionally hot, marking the third warmest summer in Southern states since records began. Conversations buzzed about the weather and climate change. Families in the northern city areas flocked to swimming lakes in the foothills, while those in more affluent southern neighbourhoods maximized their time in private swimming pools.

In the downtown business district, work proceeded as usual within air-conditioned office buildings. The hum of the air-conditioners in competition with the song of the local birds. Nearby, in the upscale Walks shopping district, shop owners collaborated to introduce a misting system along the sidewalk, ensuring a pleasant shopping experience despite the summer heat. Nestled almost at the center of the Walks, between the Tory Burch shop and an upscale kitchen store, is the "Purple Orchid," an upscale nail salon. Adorned with bougainvillea and orchids, the salon has a stellar reputation in the city, albeit with a higher price tag. Throughout the summer, the salon bustled with activity and conversations centered around the weather and strategies to beat the heat. There was always gossip about celebrities and people in the public eye, with people voicing different opinions. However, on the afternoon of August 23, the starting point of our story, the repartee took a different turn when the customers discussed Meghan Markle, even though Jinni, the Thai owner of the salon, did not know who she was.

On that date, Meghan Markle, the Duchess of Sussex, had released a podcast on Spotify ostensibly discussing female ambition. Meghan, an American actress turned Duchess upon marrying Prince Harry of England, was, in August 2022, a divisive figure on both sides of the Atlantic. This stemmed largely from an interview they had given to Oprah Winfrey in March 2021. In this interview Meghan and Prince Harry alleged that the royal family had inclinations of racism that were directed towards her. Overlooking of course the £32 million wedding given to her and the many more concessions provided to her to make her feel welcomed, Meghan went onto to proclaim to the world via Oprah, that this mistreatment negatively affected her mental health to such a degree that on one occasion before an event with her husband at the Royal Albert Theatre, she contemplated the unthinkable. Meghan claims this prompted her husband to initiate a departure from not only Royal duties but also from England. This rather swift exodus conceived and executed by the pair, concealed from the rest of the family until the last minute, was given the name "Megxit" by the British tabloid press for the public's consumption. So off they went, first to Canada and then to California just before Covid in 2020.

Settled in California, first in a borrowed home in Beverly Hills and then in their own home in Montecito, the couple had secured multimillion-dollar contracts with Spotify and Netflix. This led to speculation in the British Press that the promise and lure of making millions was the true reason for the couples' departure from the UK and their narrative about suffering mental health crises and racism were simply fiction for their ruse.

So why not take a break and come and walk with me through the doorway surrounded by bougainvillea and enter into the Purple Orchid nail salon where you can experience the almost intoxicating bouquet of exotic flowers and not only get a masterful manicure/pedicure but also partake in the gossip of the day? You will be made very welcome by Jinni, the owner who will greet you and Amara, her niece who will give you a manicure. You can sit next to Ellie, an Englishwoman who is sat to your left or Janine, an artist who is sat to your right. Each one has a story to tell. These are their stories, narrated in their own words – stories of experiences and challenges encountered when venturing beyond one's comfort zone and mixing with people from different backgrounds and cultures…

An ambitious woman - Jinni

Hello, dear. I'm sitting here, reflecting on another long day in my nail salon – and goodness, what a day it's been. A day where the conversation took such a turn, that I became concerned what might happen if any government officials were to overhear. But I am getting ahead of myself……

The staff have just left, and now it's just me, sitting here, finally relaxing. Picture me with my feet up, sipping a tiny bit of SangSom – the most delicious Thai rum. You should try it; it will blow your socks off!

As I sit here, I can still smell the beautiful flowers that fill my salon – lotus, orchids, and jasmines today. All flowers that grow in Thailand and remind me of home with their beauty and scents.

Then there's the large picture of a fishing boat at Koh Samui – a reminder of my homeland and the beautiful beaches. I love these reminders of home but I also love living here; America has been good to me. Lots of lovely money. You Americans just love my manicures and pedicures. It seems a long time now since we were closed due to Covid restrictions, and times were hard.

But I am forgetting myself; I was going to tell you about today – my goodness, where to start! The salon was full this afternoon – many people are regulars, and every seat was taken. Today we had a new visitor to the salon – an English woman called Ellie. Her appointment was being paid for by a regular of mine, Jenni, who it turned out was her mother-in-law.

Ellie seemed a bit dowdy to me, but she was wearing a beautiful diamond ring, and she said she wanted a manicure to show it off. I always do Janine's nails – she is a beautiful black lady who is an artist. So, I sat Ellie down next to us and got Amara to do her nails. That cute Kara was at the other side having a pedicure – how that appalling man could have left her for another woman is beyond me; she is such a sweetheart.

It wasn't long before Ellie started talking about a podcast she had been listening to, and the people in it. I could sense that Janine was bristling, and soon she was joining in. They seemed to be talking about the British Royal Family, and not in a favourable way. This frightened me because in my country, we are not allowed to criticize the royal family – people caught engaging in criticism can go to prison for up to 15 years.

I became scared, worrying that my nail salon might become a hotbed of political intrigue, and I might lose the business I have worked so hard for! What if one of the customers was a government official and turned me in for allowing such talk?

At this time, I wasn't 100% sure they were talking about real people. I know Americans love to discuss soap operas and movies they watch; they talk about the characters as if they were real. Perhaps this was all made up? It certainly seemed far-fetched. They also seemed to be talking about racism, and this really threw me. There is no talk of racism in my salon. I felt I had to get involved to try to find out what they were talking about and shut it down if necessary.

I spoke up saying to them - this podcast you have been listening to doesn't make sense to me, especially the married couple you have been talking about.

They both looked at me and asked why? So, I went on. I said - from what I heard you say about this married couple - she is a divorced American woman who had an acting part in a soap opera and then went to England and married him, and he just happens to be a British Prince who is a multi-millionaire. His granny, the Queen, gave them a 30-million-dollar wedding, the bride wore jewels and Givenchy couture, and they stayed in castles. But the British were evil racists because the bride's mother was black, and the bride was an ambitious American woman. The multi-millionaire prince wanted to help her, so he got men who were even richer than him to help. A Russian oligarch gave them a house to live in on an island in Canada for a time, and then an American film producer who felt her pain let them live in his Beverly Hills mansion for free, and then Spotify and Netflix gave them hundreds of millions of dollars to dish the dirt on his evil racist family back in England.

Janine said – that is very good Jinni – that is right about the background of the couple. But why does it not make sense?

So I said – but it is an unbelievable story – surely nobody would believe in characters like that – they are obviously made up – it is too far-fetched to be true! I then mimed hearing a noise and said - Oh excuse me – that is my phone ringing – it is a billionaire prince who feels my pain and is going to take me away from all this on his private jet to a desert island. I finished that up by laughing loudly.

Well dear no-one else laughed - there was this silence – honestly you could hear a pin drop – everybody in the salon stopped and looked at me.

Janine said – it's not made-up Jinni – what you just said is the true story of Meghan Markle and Prince Harry of England – the Duke and Duchess of Sussex. You must have heard of them – everybody in the world has been talking about them!

Ellie said – yes and now Markle is talking about it all on her boring podcast!

Kara said – a podcast Spotify is paying 30 million dollars for her to produce and star in.

Suddenly the whole salon erupted, and everyone was talking about Markle and Prince Harry while I sat there with a very red face. They all knew something about them – Markle's outrageous gowns, the invisible children, Elton John lent them his private jet, and on and on and on....

I said loudly "Please stop!!! You should not be discussing the British Royal Family in such a disrespectful way. These people are Royalty, and as such, we must respect them. To not respect them is to court trouble with the government."

Ellie said "We do not have to respect them – we can say what we like!!"

Janine said "Jinni, why do you feel we will be making trouble with the government by talking about the British Royal Family? – for goodness sake you are in America now! We have the First Amendment here – freedom of speech!"

I sat there staring at them feeling like a fish that was out of water. I will never understand these people as long as I live, I swear! Freedom of speech? I thought about my niece Arpa in Thailand and her involvement in the fight for free speech within the country, and my heart ached for her.

Janine got her phone out (mid manicure) and showed me pictures of the Duke and Duchess of Sussex.

My goodness – if I am allowed First Amendment rights as someone living in the USA - all I could think was: Is that a British Prince? What a mucky pup!! They were reclining under a tree, and he lay there with a big bare foot in the forefront of the picture – the sole was on view for all to see and it looked dirty! You see dear, as a professional, I am always concerned with hands and feet, and he lies there sticking his great big grubby foot into the camera!! Euuuw! I wonder if he would be interested in my pedicure for the discerning gentleman – I could even treble the price, as he could afford to pay.

So I here I sit sipping the SangSom and getting ready to make the journey to my apartment in the northern suburbs. I wonder to myself what I should cook this evening. I decide I will do Pad Thai noodles as that is quick and easy and always delicious.

Cooking Thai food and eating always calms me so that I am ready for the next day....

Pad Thai recipe

This spicy treat is relatively easy to cook if you are organised and treat it as three key phases. Prepare the sauce first so that you are not having to measure things out as you go. The recipe has been split roughly into sections for carbs, sauce and protein.

The carbs for this recipe come from vermicelli rice noodles. These can be cooked shortly ahead of the main cooking and rinsed in cold water to cool.

Sauce ingredients:

Fish sauce 3 tbs
Soy sauce 1 tbs
Brown sugar 3 tbs
Rice vinegar 2 tbs
Sriracha hot sauce 1 tbs
Combine the sauce ingredients and set aside

Veggie ingredients:
1 thinly sliced red pepper
3 minced garlic cloves
Bean sprouts
3 green onions, thinly sliced
2 limes
coriander

Protein
4 ounces of raw shrimp
2 eggs, beaten
Handful of peanuts, chopped or whole

Method

After cooking the noodles and making the sauce, beat the eggs and set aside.

Heat 2 tbs of peanut oil in a wide pan or wok.

Add the shrimp, garlic and red pepper. Stir fry briefly, until the shrimp have turned pink on both sides. This should only take a few minutes.

Push the mixture to one side of the pan and then add the beaten eggs, stirring rapidly with a spatula until they have scrambled into smallish pieces.

Add the sauce mixture, beansprouts peanuts and noodles. Toss together to combine.

Top the finished dish with the green onions and chopped coriander leaves. Squeeze the juice of a half lime over the dish and add a few lime wedges to garnish.

"When comfort has stifled ambition - Ellie"

It has been quite an unusual day, unlike my usual routine, and I find myself compelled to put pen to paper before the details slip from memory. As an adjunct faculty member at the university, I often encourage my students to reflect and record their emotions, so it's only fitting that I follow my own advice and candidly document my feelings.

I'm an Englishwoman living in the United States, sharing my life with my American husband, Kevin. At this very moment, he peacefully snoozes in the Barca lounger, and I can't help but smile at his tranquillity. Our journey began in England, where Kevin pursued his master's degree, and fate had us on the same course. Later, he embarked on a Ph.D., while I decided to abandon further studies. We both found teaching positions at a former polytechnic in Birmingham, and life was comfortable. Our earnings were substantial, and we enjoyed financial stability, making me question the necessity of further academic pursuits.

In 2019, Kevin's father passed away in America, prompting his desire to return and be closer to his mother. We had $200,000 from the sale of our Birmingham house, which we used as a down payment on a home here. However, housing costs in the U.S. are considerably higher, leading to a significant mortgage. Kevin secured a permanent full-time job at the local university, benefiting from his Ph.D. qualifications. In contrast, I discovered that the only available teaching position for someone without a Ph.D. is as adjunct faculty. While it may sound promising, it's more akin to the gig economy within academia. I receive payment per course I teach, with little to no advance notice, no job security, and no benefits, all while working tirelessly for meagre compensation.

In fact, I currently teach at two universities to make ends meet. The State University (where Kevin also works) and a small private college outside of the city. This leaves me with a gruelling four-day workweek, dashing all over town. Today, however, was a rare day off.

The constant commuting and financial constraints often lead us to opt for fast food like McDonald's or Taco Bell for dinner. Regrettably, both Kevin and I have seen our waistlines expand, marking just one of the many signs of a general decline.

Today began with a coffee meetup with my mother-in-law, Jenni. I had received a beautiful diamond ring from my late Auntie Betty's estate, and I was eager to wear it for the first time and show it to Jenni. Now, don't get me wrong, Jenni is a lovely lady, but the moment I see her, my initial thought is, "It's not fair!" How can a woman in her sixties look so incredibly good? I realize this isn't the right way to think about your mother-in-law, but her appearance consistently left me feeling inadequate. Today, she was donning white pants and a form-fitting top, radiating confidence. In contrast, I was clad in my latest purchase from Target – a pair of jeans with an elasticated waist and a top designed to hide any imperfections.

As my mind wandered, I couldn't help but remember the last time we met. Kevin and I had visited her house for a poolside barbecue. Jenni had invited her boyfriend, Niall, a man younger than her, often referred to as a "toyboy." By any standards, he was remarkably attractive. That day, I discreetly glanced at my beloved Kevin, ten years younger than Niall, but exhibiting the tell-tale signs of a growing belly and a double chin. I spent the afternoon firmly planted on a lounger, acutely conscious of my own body, focusing on perceived flaws, from thunder thighs to a flabby stomach.

Jenni is always kind, which can sometimes be infuriating. On this day, she complimented my new ring and treated me to a manicure at the Purple Orchid salon which she had prepaid for me. By the time I boarded the train to the salon, I was inexplicably in a foul mood, despite the new ring and the luxury of a manicure. My irritation seemed unwarranted, yet I couldn't shake it.

I turned to Spotify, hoping to improve my mood, but I made the mistake of tuning into a new podcast by Meghan Markle. She has a knack for getting on my nerves, even under the best circumstances. For some reason, I decided to listen. It didn't take long for me to become incensed. Meghan was lamenting that she had never considered ambition a negative trait until she moved to England and married Prince Harry. She referred to him as her "now" husband an expression which I found irritating. I interpreted it as she believed that the English disliked ambitious women, which didn't sit well with me. In a moment of exasperation, I nearly shouted my thoughts aloud on the train.

By the time I reached the salon, my disposition had worsened. It seemed ridiculous to be in such a state, especially when a manicure was such a rare treat for me. The manicurist, Amara, noticed my English background and asked about my experiences living in the

United States, curious about any differences. I launched into a discussion about the podcast and expressed my opinion on Meghan Markle, which led to an unexpected debate with another customer, a beautiful black lady sitting beside me. She appeared to take offense at my perspective, and we were on the brink of a heated discussion. However, the salon owner, Jinni, shocked me when she said that in Thailand you are not allowed to discuss the Royal Family in a disrespectful way. This turned the conversation - we told her that she was in the USA now and here you can discuss what you wish – there is freedom of speech. Soon, we found ourselves laughing and sharing anecdotes about the royal couple instead.

As I left the salon, the two ladies, Janine and Kara, who had been sitting next to me, left simultaneously. We were still in high spirits, and Janine suggested getting coffee together to continue our discussion about the royal duo. We all agreed and headed to a nearby coffee shop. There, we spent a delightful half-hour conversing, sharing laughter, and getting to know each other better. We decided to meet up again in a couple of weeks and exchanged phone numbers.

I boarded the train home in a much better mood and decided to send a message to my friend Barbara in England. However, when I opened WhatsApp, I was surprised to find a message from Niall, my mother-in-law's boyfriend. It struck me as somewhat unusual, and the message read, "Hello Ellie. How are you? I enjoyed meeting you at the BBQ last week. I hope you don't mind me writing – I got your number from Jenni. Jenni tells me you teach statistics, and I really need some help with a presentation I must make. I wondered if we could meet for a coffee, and you could assist me?" The request seemed innocent enough, but my thoughts about Niall were anything but innocent.

Reflecting on the message, I glanced at Kevin, who had now reached the crescendo of his snoring, and pondered my next steps.

What should I do? I now had two new friends to consult for advice.

An ambitious, well-travelled woman – Janine.

It is a warm summer evening, and I am by the pool, sipping a glass of wine, eager for my granny to pick up the phone. I can't wait to share today's events. The comments from Jinni at the nail salon about not being allowed to discuss the Thai Royal Family due to a perceived lack of respect shock me. As an American, I grew up with the belief in the right to freedom of speech granted by our constitution. The idea that Jinni couldn't freely express herself in her own country of Thailand was startling. I wanted to discuss this with my nan...

My interest in the British Royal Family, especially Prince Harry's marriage to Meghan Markle, connects me with Meghan on a personal level. We are both black women who moved to England in 2017. Meghan's fairy tale of moving from Canada as an actress to live with her Prince is captivating. In contrast, my journey involved my husband Gene, a Certified Public Accountant (CPA) at Alex Gold, an international firm of accountants. Gene had been given a two-year opportunity to work in the London office starting in 2017. I, an artist and furniture designer, joined him to explore design in London. I was particularly interested in some of the work by African artists in London. I was also lucky enough to visit Africa during this time to further my interest in African art.

Despite my love for England, the cultural shift was sometimes challenging. The size of the apartments (or "flats") for rent was surprising, but we opted for a hall floor flat in a Georgian listed building. The grandeur of the old buildings came with drawbacks like noise between floors. Meghan and Prince Harry, despite the millions spent on Frogmore Cottage, didn't escape their share of challenges. Frogmore Cottage is situated on the Royal Family's Windsor Estate and is not as grand as some of the castles the family live in. London's multicultural atmosphere, historical landmarks, and traditions, like the changing of the guard at Windsor Castle, were highlights...

Reflecting on Meghan's entry into the Royal Family, I was in England during her 2018 wedding. The Royal Family spared no expense, and Gene and I watched on TV. Gene, being an accountant, noted the wealthy guests and had some cynical thoughts about their motives. He even foresaw the potential for exclusive interviews. In retrospect, I wonder if Gene saw things I didn't...

Of course, much has happened since Meghan and Prince Harry's time in England. They left in December 2019 to live first in Canada and then the USA. Gene and I also left England at about the same time to return to the USA. Gene was promoted to senior manager at Alex Gold, CPAs, and I started work in a Cooperative in downtown where I had as my specialty African Art.

Since living in the USA, Meghan and Prince Harry had taken part in the Oprah Winfrey interview and

signed lucrative deals with Netflix and Spotify. Today's Spotify podcast, part of their deal, intrigued me, and I wanted to discuss it with my granny.

As the phone rings for a WhatsApp video call with Granny, we share a light moment seeing Roger, her dog, looking into the camera. Granny, shocked by the restrictions on criticizing the Royal Family in Thailand, emphasizes our fortune in having the freedom to speak up...

Granny seems reserved about Meghan's podcast, expressing concern about her dominating conversations... She then continues by telling me about her friend Amy's accident. What a saga that was! Amy at 72 is older than granny by a couple of years and they are both widows living alone. Last week Amy fell in the bedroom and could not get up again. She had to crawl across the room on her hands and knees to get to her phone. By the time she reached her phone she was exhausted. It was midnight and she didn't know who to ring. In the end, she rang Joyce next door. Joyce didn't have a key to the house and Amy was upstairs in the bedroom with the door locked! In the end the paramedics had to come round to break the door down to get in and go upstairs to help Amy to get up. She had a brief visit to the hospital where she was checked over. The doctor told her it was her "core" that was weak. He explained that your core is the central part of your body and includes the lower back, pelvis, hips and stomach. He said that core muscles are needed to help with balance and strength. If core muscles are weak then you may experience back pain and muscle injuries. Also, if you fall you may not be strong enough to get up again. He said it was a problem with ageing. Amy has been very worried about this and as she lives alone with no family in the city, she knows she has to be able to look after herself. Amy and granny had talked about this, and they both decided they should work to strengthen their core and to get fit. Amy's doctor had told her he would work with her to develop a fitness plan. This would include some training with weights, cardio training with an online instructor (Robert John) and he suggested running. Granny was happy to join in on this plan and was going to see her doctor if he would agree to her taking part. She was especially concerned to find out if she should start running at her age. She had booked an appointment in the following week.

Later, as we get ready for bed, I tell Gene about Amy's fall and Granny's interest in getting fit over the Spotify podcast. Gene, with his humorous take, comments on the allure of working out compared to Meghan Markle imparting wisdom to the world...

When ambition leaves - Amara

As the day at Auntie Jinnipha's nail salon ended, filled with nail painting, filing, and polite conversations with customers, I realized Dad wasn't there to pick me up as planned. Instead, I booked and paid in advance for an Uber to get home. When I arrived, my mom had exciting news to share – Keesha, our neighbor and childhood friend, had landed a role in a cable TV show, and her performance was being praised. Keesha had left our small town for the bustling city.

It's hard to believe that just six months ago, my life was worlds apart from what it is today. I was in my second year at UCLA, deeply engrossed in studying politics, philosophy, and economics. The world seemed full of opportunities, and I was the first in my family to attend university, consistently earning straight A's. My dad, an immigrant from Thailand, had an erratic work schedule, while my mom's family had run a thriving bakery in town. Using her inheritance following my grandad's passing, my mom purchased our current residence in the Southern Hills development – a magnificent four-bedroom, five-bathroom house complete with a pool and stunning city views, an estate agent's dream.

My scholarship to UCLA covered tuition and part of my living expenses, and life was good for a while. Then, the fateful decisions came. After I celebrated my 21st birthday I started to go to bars regularly. One night I went to a bar on Santa Monica Blvd, where I met Brett, a charismatic cameraman with extravagant tales about his work, including a temporary stint on the Ellen show during Meghan Markle's controversial appearance. However, Brett's extravagant spending habits and my neglect of my studies led to academic setbacks. I moved in with him, took on a job at the bar, and accumulated credit card debt.

As my studies suffered, I pushed myself further away from success, despite my personal tutor, Dr. Benkleton, offering guidance. Overwhelmed by guilt and failing exams, I severed communication with Dr. Benkleton and hit rock bottom. I ended up dropping out of university. Mom and Dad had to pick me up, and the car ride home was filled with my mom's audible disappointment. Two months were spent languishing in bed, and Brett became a part of my past.

My mom did her best to clear my debts, but Dad's drinking habits escalated, and I blamed myself for their strained relationship. Luckily, Auntie Jinni extended a helping hand and offered me a job at the salon. I trained as a nail technician, where I spent my days politely serving customers. Mom, once a diligent bakery worker, had transitioned to an administrative role at the local TV station. Despite her behind-the-scenes position, she remained star-struck. Later that evening, I found her captivated by the show she had mentioned earlier, featuring Keesha. She praised Keesha's acting abilities and recollected our joint venture signing up with Elite's talent agency when we were teenagers. Keesha had taken advantage of this signing and I had not, in mom's estimation.

Mom pressed me about my future, but I cut her off, expressing disinterest in an acting career. She reminded me of my resistance to being a student, and she labelled my life as a "disaster."

As we shared dinner, I noticed Dad's tired eyes. After the meal, I retreated to my room, anticipating their argument. The weight of depression settled in, and I reflected on my mistakes, fearing the monotony of another day at the salon. I questioned whether my inability to concentrate might be a sign of a mental issue. Seeking answers, I turned to YouTube and came across a Doctor Phil episode about an adult son still dependent on his parents, a topic that hit close to home.

Chapter 2

The end of summer

By the end of August, there had been 60 consecutive days of 90 degree plus temperature. Everyone longed for the cooler weather. There had been hurricanes in the mid-west and there were rumours that a tornado might be heading for the city.

Despite the heat a real estate boom in the city continued unabated. In the Southern Hills development, for the first time a home sold for more than $1 million to an anonymous buyer. Prices rose in the northern suburbs pricing many families out of the popular Brighton Rock with its proximity to the city centre and transport links. Areas began to change and become gentrified.

The local TV and radio stations were full of news about the real estate boom. The Purple Orchid nail salon had invested in a series of adverts on the local radio station, and these had been a huge success. The popularity of the salon continued to grow, so fast that it was now advisable to book well in advance for a session. People came to the salon from all areas of the city and there was now a real mix of people having their nails done. Still only a few were men who came for a pedicure, but there were so many women from very different backgrounds - business women, teachers, nurses, doctors, attorneys, actresses and artists to name just a few.

Ellie's mother-in-law Jenni had now agreed to pay for her to have a manicure every couple of weeks. These visits usually coincided with Janine and Kara's appointments and the three enjoyed having coffee together afterwards.

Meghan Markle released another podcast in her series on Spotify. This podcast was about divas and Mariah Carey was her guest. Meghan talked about her own ethnicity. A mixture of black and white, but in her view, only treated as a black woman when she married her English husband. She became quite upset when she felt that Mariah Carey had called her a diva.

I started to sweat a little bit. I started squirming in my chair in this quiet revolt, like, wait, wait, no, what? How? How could you? That's not true, that's not."

This podcast again stimulated conversation in the salon, but this time Jinni knew who Meghan was but was still somewhat too constrained by her cultural beliefs to join in .....

A heart to heart in the back room of the salon - Jinni

Let me sit down first before I talk this evening. I am just exhausted. Of course, I want to be busy in the salon, it is my business, and I am making a good profit! But today I have been run off my feet – including six pedicures.

After the embarrassment of not knowing who the Duke and Duchess of Sussex were, I have now read up on them. I know all about them leaving England and moving first to Canada and then to the USA. So, curiosity piqued, I went ahead, and I actually listened to Meghan Markle talking to Mariah Carey on her latest podcast. Now let me confide my feelings to you dear in confidence. This is not for discussion in the salon! My oh my I have huge respect for that Mariah Carey – Meghan could hardly get a word in – Mariah certainly stood her corner!! She also called Meghan a diva. What a woman. I would do Mariah's pedicure for free – even if she had been dancing around on the stage for hours at one of her concerts sweating buckets.

I go online and see my niece Arpa is waiting to talk to me. I love to speak to her. She lives in Bangkok with her partner and is working hard to establish a career. When she was at university, she took part in the 2020 protests in Bangkok. Protestors attempted to march on the parliament. The parliament was debating making changes to the constitution. The march took place as the activists were concerned that parliament would dismiss the changes and in particular demands that there be reform in the monarchy. During the march I understand that they threw bags of paint and smoke bombs at the police who then turned a water cannon on them. Taking part in a march is not something I would ever do and I fear for Arpa that she got involved. I know she is still an activist, so I worry about her.

I ask how she is, and we exchange pleasantries about the weather and her family.

I then tell her about the incident in the Salon when everyone was discussing the Duke and Duchess of Sussex and how worried I was as they are still members of the British royal family. Although they are non-working royals, they should still be treated with respect.

But, I say, to be honest, dear, I find it hard to understand the pair of them. In our country Thailand, you can be sent to prison for disrespecting the King. Also, recently a courtier was found to be upstaging the Queen and she had her Royal Titles removed. This shows the strength of our Royal Family. Yet here we have Meghan Markle, an American woman, who married into the British Royal Family and then accused them of being racists! She did this on television in a programme shown in the USA and UK and watched by millions – and nothing happened. The pair still have their titles. I really wonder about the British Royal Family – have they no backbone? How could they allow this to happen? Meghan is having a laugh surely? Or at least becoming rich at the expense of his family. What a funny old world we live in. Perhaps they all deserve the disrespect of their own countrymen like Ellie, a customer of mine who was really running them down.

Arpa nodded and said: She agreed that in Thailand it would be wrong to speak about the Royal Family in such a way, but she also felt that freedom of speech is a wonderful thing. It is one of the things that she has been fighting for, all during her time at university and continuing now. It is wrong to have to speak in private and not be able to air our views in public she said.

I don't know if I agree with her or not. What is the point of being able to air your views if they are ignored? Best to keep quiet and show respect. I decided to steer the conversation to more safe topics, so we talked for a while comfortably about new recipes, the price of food and a new car Arpa had bought which had turned out to be a bit of a disaster.

When Arpa left, I sat staring into the darkness in the room contemplating how far I was from all I knew in my homeland. But wait -oh my goodness! Excuse me for a moment. I have got a visitor. It is my brother, Somchai, carrying a bottle of SangSom. I get the glasses and he pours us each a glass full. He looks like he may have had a few already. Just to fill you in on his background, he is married to an American woman called Barb. He met Barb when she visited Bangkok years ago. They have been married 22 years and Amara, who works in the salon, is their daughter. I find Barb rather difficult to get along with. She is a rich American and very loud and full of her own importance. When her father died, she bought a house in the Southern Hills development with the inheritance money. It is a very big fancy place, dear. Somchai loves living there and acting like he is King of the Castle for most of the time...... the rest of the time he is miserable and drunk. If I am going to be honest, I prefer to live in a one-bedroom apartment in the north side of the city rather than put up with Barb.

Somchai wants to confide about his family. He swirls the SangSom in his glass and pauses to drink and then pours more as he talks.

Amara is not getting on with her mother – she is sulky and doesn't speak during meals.

Barb has paid off Amara's debts from her time at UCLA and Amara is not grateful.

Barb wastes money all the time – on her hair, her nails (!!!!), and Botox which Somchai thinks is ridiculous plus she is now on a course of Ozempic, not for diabetes, but to control her weight.

I bite my tongue when he says she is wasting money on her nails – of course, she isn't, she comes here, and her nails look fabulous!

He sits quietly before pouring another SangSom and leaning across the table tells me the thing that is really bothering him. Barb has been too tired and busy with work to (as he puts it) "care" about him for so long now he has forgotten when the last time was. He can't put up with it much longer – it is messing with his head. He then confides that sex with Barb has not been good for a long time now. He feels she is just going through the motions, and she is not really into it. She prefers watching the Late Show nowadays.

I sit and let him ramble on as I know what is coming next. True to form he leans over the table and slurring slightly tells me about Randi, one of the hostesses at the Black Cat bar. It seems Randi really likes sex and makes him feel like a real man in bed. She can't wait to get her hands on him to hear him talk. The problem is he has nowhere to invite her to where they can be intimate……

I know I shouldn't encourage him…. I know I should tell him to behave and go back to Barb…..but I always end up giving in to him no matter how wrong it is. So it is, after he has drunk another couple SangSoms I have agreed that he can go to my apartment early tomorrow evening. I will eat dinner out after work before returning late in the evening when they have left.

He is slurring and staggering slightly as we walk out of the salon after I have called and paid for two Ubers later in the evening – one to a mansion in the Southern Hills and one to a one room apartment in the nameless northern suburbs. As I settle into my Uber I look forward to the quiet and solitude of my place where I can warm up a green curry from a batch I cooked earlier in the week and watch the Late Show ready for another very busy day tomorrow.

Niall confides in Ellie

It's the end of August and we are already back into classes. Another difference between the USA and my old life in England. In the UK classes didn't start after the summer until the end of September so I had a nice long break in the summer. In one way it is good we are back as I am only paid when I teach so it means more money. I am teaching 2 classes at the State University this term and one class at a small Catholic university 25 miles away. Kevin has a permanent position at the State University, so we usually go together in his car when I teach there.

Today the traffic is heavy, and we inch along the freeway with the air con on at maximum. I have messaged Kara and Janine about Niall asking for my help with a presentation. They both encouraged me to meet Niall and I have arranged a meeting in a coffee shop in town tomorrow. I mention this to Kevin.

Kevin seems dismissive "Is this about his band "The Brothers of Swing"?" he asks.

When I say I am not sure he goes on "I bet it is about his band – what else has he got? What a loser the guy is! That band will never make any money covering old classics and I am sure he knows it. He doesn't make much teaching people to drive either. My poor old mom is being taken for a sucker with him".

I bristle at these comments "Kevin that is a bit unfair – your mom seems very happy with Niall, and you don't know that he doesn't make any money".

Kevin snorts "I can spot a grifter when I see one – and that guy is one. He needs to up his qualifications and get a real job".

I give up – I have never known Kevin like this. I saw him as a gentle soul when I met him in England. Big and cuddly with a mop of dark hair – I just wanted to be held by him. He was like a big cuddly bear. I wondered if he was jealous of Niall?

We lapsed into silence as we inched along the freeway.

Finally, we arrived at the campus and Kevin went to his office on the 10th floor of the Brechard building reminding me as he left that we were going to the gym as soon as we finish work. Jenni had paid for us each a gym membership. As I said she is very kind - Kevin was enjoying the gym, but to be honest I hated it. I came out red faced and exhausted.

I rushed off to my first class and then the day went by very quickly as I was busy either teaching or spending time helping students with their queries. For the few minutes that I was free I went along to the office I shared with other adjunct faculty. What a joke this office was! You went into the basement of the Brechard building and then walked down a long corridor with exposed heating pipes as far as you could go and there was the windowless office. We hot desked, which meant that you did not have your own desk. You sat at whichever desk was vacant when you went into the room. So, if you got there at the wrong time you might not even get somewhere to sit. Today only a colleague Ron was in the office so there was room for me to sit. I got my laptop out and looked up the Thai Royal Family on the internet. I had been intrigued by Jinni's reaction when we discussed the Duke and Duchess of Sussex. Today I read up about their law of "lese-majeste". This law meant that you could go to prison for up to 15 years for disrespecting the Thai Royal Family. It was quite shocking to me as I suppose I had taken the right to free speech as a given and had not realised that this was not true the world over.

The least said about the gym in the evening the better!! I went to the Zumba class. Dancing around in leggings and a tight top I looked like a fairy elephant in the mirrors of the gym. Not only did I look ungainly I could not keep up with the dance steps! My face was bright red, and I sounded like a steam train!! I didn't want to talk to anyone but the woman next to me smiled and seemed to be sympathetic to how I felt.

The next day I was due to meet Niall for a coffee to discuss the presentation. I spent some time after showering applying make-up and picking out a nice summer dress. I sprayed myself with Hermes "Eau des Merveilles Bleue" – an extravagant purchase at duty free on the flight from the UK. That plus bright red lipstick and I was ready to meet Niall. When I saw him in the coffee shop, he looked even more handsome than I had remembered. I was worried that I was blushing as I said Hi. We ordered coffees and sat in a quiet corner. It turned out, Kevin was correct the presentation was about Niall's band "The Brothers of Swing" . After opening pleasantries, Niall was all business.

Niall said: We have played together for about 5 years now. There are 3 of us -me, Ronnie and Pete. We play at weddings and bar mitzvahs. We also play at venues in the downtown area and further afield. We started out doing covers of Frank Sinatra, Dean Martin and other classics. We dress in tuxes. We get paid every time we perform but there is no set rate, and we have to accept what the venue wants to pay us.

We knew there was not much of a future performing cover songs. A couple of years ago, we decided to write some of our own songs. Ronnie and I wrote a song which went down really well when we performed it live so we put together enough for an album. People loved our songs and Pete's son filmed a video of us singing which we put up on YouTube. We had over 50,000 views so we wondered if we could go further? At this time, we were not making enough to give up the day jobs. We found out that we could sign up with a distributor called "Music world" who would upload our music onto major streaming services including Spotify and Apple Music. We paid a basic fee, and they released our music to the streamers. We were told we would make money every time it is streamed or downloaded. We were enthusiastic about this, but then we found out just how little we would be paid! Do you know we get paid less than one cent per stream?

Niall mentioned a new union called the United Musicians and Allied Workers Union that he was thinking of joining. But few musicians were organised and in a union. At the moment, musicians he felt, were at the mercy of venues and streaming services that could pay what they want!

He told me that he is going to make a presentation at a meeting of local musicians to encourage them to work together to try to get more money out of the streaming service. He asked for my help to make his presentation grab the attention of those attending. I told him I would be delighted to help.

Niall mentions that the band are playing at "The Twisted Oak" on Saturday night and he invited Kevin and I to go and watch and to bring Jenni along.

I am looking forward to Saturday night and to hear "The Brothers of Swing" and to helping Niall with his presentation.

Janine talks to Amara about being mixed race in America

I haven't been able to get Jinni out of my mind since that day in the salon when it came out that in Thailand you cannot talk about the Royal Family in a disrespectful way. I think freedom of speech is something I have always taken for granted and it seems shocking to me. I have been reading up about the Thai Royal Family on the internet and it seems there is a lot to talk about. The present King took his entourage to Germany (Bavaria) when Covid started and stayed in a hotel there rather than in his own country. I read he took many mistresses with him. He is also fabulously wealthy – I wonder where he got the money from.

The next time I went to the salon I wondered what I should and should not discuss so as not to offend Jinni and her niece Amara. They were full of gossip – first Jinni – about the real estate boom in the city and then Amara – about Meghan Markle's podcast with Mariah Carey. Amara was very impressed with Mariah Carey who she felt could "really handle herself". Amara and Mariah are both mixed race.

I had arranged to go for a coffee after my appointment with Ellie and Kara and we invited Amara to join us. I was really interested to find out from Amara what it was like to be mixed race. I knew her father was Thai and her mother was American. This gave her a rich and diverse background.

I am African American I said. But my family has never forgotten our African heritage. I explained that when I was growing up my parents had encouraged me to explore my African roots.

However, this was not easy. My ancestors came to America on slave ships and there were no immigration records for these people. In recent years with the advent of DNA it had gotten easier. If you take a simple saliva test this can help show what region of Africa your ancestors come from even if it is not possible to see immigration records. We had done this to find out my family had their roots in Nigeria. However, we had then gone on to the Ancestry website and found out that there were census records from 1870 which included African Americans by name and we were able to find our ancestors. We traced our ancestors back to plantations by using slave schedules. We also looked at interviews with former slaves and found one with an ancestor of ours who had worked on a plantation in Virginia. It was fascinating and the Ancestory website was very helpful. I felt it was important to know about my ancestors' lives and find out what they endured.

Amara was very quiet and was staring at me. I then asked her what she knew about her Thai roots?

Amara looked at me as if she thought I was a bit strange – she said I am American I was born here. My mom met my dad in Bangkok and then they moved back here. I just see myself as American. Auntie Jinni still follows Thai customs – but dad is happy to just do whatever my mom wants to do. He sometimes cooks Thai food for us, but most of the time we eat meatloaf, steaks, burgers like the rest of the American population.

I was quite surprised. Can you speak Thai? I asked. Amara shook her head. When I was little my dad taught me a few words, but I was not really interested. None of my friends at school were Thai so I did not see the point.

I hope I hid my feelings as I was quite shocked by this. Have you visited Thailand? I asked her. Amara said that when she was younger, she used to go to Koh Samui on vacation with her mom while her dad went "up country" to visit his relatives. His relatives in Thailand did not approve of dad marrying a white woman so mom was not welcome at the family home. Mom enjoyed laying out by the pool at the hotel sipping cocktails and Amara used to play in the pool or on the beach. The hotel was a 5-star international hotel so they talked to other Americans or Brits who were staying there, Amara explained.

Once, said Amara, we went to a shack on the beach to eat real Thai food. She pulled a face as she explained what a disaster that was. Both she and her mom were violently ill when they got back to the room!! Yuck!!

It was quite an eye opener talking to Amara – she saw herself as American and her Thai heritage seemed to have been forgotten.

Later when Gene and I were sitting up in bed reading I told him about Amara and how she had not embraced the culture of her father's country. Gene said he felt that it was okay that Amara felt she was American and was not interested in her father's country. America is a real melting pot he said and welcomes people from all cultures and countries - there is nothing wrong with feeling she is an American. He commented that her Thai father has lived here for years and probably sees himself as American too.

I went to sleep with very mixed feelings ....I feel so lucky to live in a country with free speech and lots of opportunities and Amara is lucky to have grown up here. But she is not interested in her father's country and culture, and this seems to me to be a loss.

I also made a note to myself to meet up soon with my Granny and her friend Amy. My granny was going to go to the doctor to find out if he felt she was in good enough health to start running. As she and her friend were in their seventies I wondered if it would be too much for them....

We are all Divas – Amara

I am still here, in Aunt Jinni's salon doing endless manicures. One thing I learned very quickly was that the best way to get good tips is to become friendly with the customers. This week I did Kara's nails. I really do like Kara though. She is older than me (in her late 30s) and has been going through a tough time. Her husband, who is a successful attorney, left her for someone not much older than me. I am 21. She is now a single mom with two girls and no career of her own.

We talk about her attending Real Estate school and studying for her license. I had flirted with the idea myself and we discuss selling real estate as a career. Kara seemed to think it was all about contacts. She had lived in the Southern Hills for several years and knew people there. Kara felt that with the current real estate boom, people might be looking to move to a bigger property. Sun Hills Realty were recruiting, and she had been for an interview. They were happy to take her on subject to her passing the exam. The house that had sold for a million dollars (well 990,000 if we are being precise) had been the listing of Bill Kurtz the manager and he hoped to sell others in that price range soon.

I thought for a moment and said I also knew people in Southern Hills who might be interested in buying a new house.

As I worked on her pedicure, I was in my own dream world. In my head I could see me driving a Porsche Cayenne along the winding roads of Southern Hills on my way to my latest listing. I am wearing an Alaia mini dress and Stuart Weitzman heels. I am hosting an open house – my listing is the blue mansion at the top of South Ravine. It is one of the biggest homes in the Southern Hills. I have sourced a buffet from “Made by Suz” and had my assistant Henry set it up in the main dining room. I have arranged for the rapper and DJ “Whoozi” to do a few sets out by the pool. Henry will be on the door to welcome viewers and meanwhile I will be out by the pool to talk about possible offers to brokers acting on behalf of very rich people.

“Mmmm I am not sure we could go for 2.1” I say” you will have to tell your client to come up to 2.5 or there is no deal”

Yes, it just might be a career I would consider….

Kara tells me that that evening she is having a rare night out with her girlfriends and asks if I want to join them. I agree – I haven’t been out for a while and need to let my hair down. Most of my friends are away at university and it has been lonely since I got back here. This group are older than me (I'm only 21) but they still seem pretty cool.

We end up going to the "Albion" and we soon got into the Tequila Slammers. We were up dancing, when a group of guys joined us, and it seemed they knew Kara and her group.

Soon Dean and I were getting close "Wow babe you are beautiful" he says. "You are not so bad yourself" I tease him. I can't see him too well in here as the lights are dimmed but he seems in good shape.

Since that evening Dean and I have met up a couple of times and last night I stayed over at his apartment. He is a 37-year-old sales manager who is recently divorced. He is full of compliments, and I love it!! Looking at him over breakfast I can see where age is beginning to catch up with him – he is a ginger, and he looks to have a comb over. I don't mind balding guys though – I just love guys who make me feel loved and cared for.

When I finally get home dad is in the kitchen making lunch and mom is sitting by the swimming pool on the phone to her cousin, Auntie Suzanne, who lives in Miami. They are talking about the soaps and mom is saying "she is brilliant, you should see her clothes, wow, she looks fabulous.... you just have to see it".

Then she sees me and says, "oh here she is – stayed out all night goodness knows where – she looks like she's been in a fight with a possum".

I am about to bolt for the safety of my bedroom when mom says goodbye and rings off.

"Where were you last night? Couldn't you at least send a text to let us know where you were? Dad and I were worried about you. I think I preferred it when you were in LA and I didn't know what you were up to! Honestly you are totally thoughtless – all you care about is yourself."

I say "sorry mom I really meant to text you, but everything is fine"

Mom "tuts tuts" for a bit and then says "Well the good news is that Keesha has a break from filming next week and she is coming home. She is such a thoughtful daughter. There is going to be a party next door to celebrate her coming home" mom pauses and seems very excited at the prospect and then says "and we are all invited."

I go up to my room and have a long, hot shower. She will have to eat her words, I think, when I am the top real estate agent in the county selling millions of dollars of real estate. When I am married to Dean with a lavish reception which we pay for ourselves at the country club. I will be wearing the most beautiful gown and we will be featured in the "Southern Hills Style" magazine.

Dreams can come true – I will show all the non-believers!!

Chapter 3

The beginning of Fall...

September arrived bringing cooler weather – a welcome relief after the heat of the summer. Families made use of the bike and hiking trails around the lakes to the north of the city.

There had been a spate of robberies and murders at the end of the summer which had shocked local residents. In Gent Town near to downtown, Lee Kona, the owner of a convenience store, fed up with robberies had shot and killed an intruder into the store. In the Southern Hills there had been a carjacking on Southern Boulevard which had turned ugly with another murder.

Despite this unpleasantness, real estate in the city continued to boom and very low unemployment was reported.

The Purple Orchid continued to be very busy – and the hours were extended from 10 am in the morning until 7 pm in the evening on 5 days per week. Saturday, the hours were 10 am until 4 pm and Sunday, the salon was closed. A new manicurist, Song, was taken on and she settled happily into the salon.

On September 5, Meghan Markle released another podcast "The Stigma of the Singleton" with Mindy Kaling. In this podcast she described herself as a child as an "ugly duckling" with a "huge gap in my teeth" and "massive frizzy curly hair". She also said that as a child she was very intelligent and smart. She also discussed the pressure women feel under to find a partner and it is only when she has been "chosen" by a man that a woman might feel she is "good enough". Ms Markle apparently was not happy with people saying how lucky she was that Prince Harry had chosen her, she argued that she had chosen him too.

Three days later, on September 8, the Queen of England died and the whole British nation went into mourning.

Jinni - A successful single woman

Each day I go to the salon and each day I give thanks that the salon is popular and busy. The new manicurist I have employed, a Chinese girl named Song, seems to be settling in well and the customers like her.

The customers want to talk while they have their nails done – and we discuss anything and everything. The cost of housing, the robberies and violence that have taken place recently in our town, celebrities. You name it we discuss it. I am still wary about discussing the British Royal Family and critiquing their behaviour in my salon. I know I can discuss them as I am in a country that has freedom of speech, yet it does not somehow feel right. I did listen to the latest Meghan Markle podcast and I don't know what it means - the stigma of the singleton. It seems to be discussing the traditional view that women should fall in love and be married to fit in. Since my divorce, I am a single woman and I manage very well, believe me. I am proud of my business and what I have achieved. What is marriage anyway? Look at my brother Somchai and his antics! What an advertisement for marriage, he is!

Over the last week or so, I have gone to "dinner" on a couple of occasions so he can take his latest "friend" Randi back to my apartment. Yesterday, I got back about 10.30 and there they were just leaving. When I saw Randi I nearly audibly sighed. Randi turns out to be a busty white woman who looks like she has had so much plastic surgery that she can hardly move her face. She is hardly in the first flush of youth! It is Barb all over again. But I do vaguely get it, this is Barb without the mouth and the attitude. Randi is simpering all over him and treating him like the "Big Man". I expect he will have told her a pack of lies about his wealth and career.

At the moment my biggest concern is for Amara. She is diligent at her duties as a manicurist, but I can see she is not happy. I wonder if she regrets giving up on her degree studies. I am not sure how to advise her. I know I really should make time to sit down with her and chat, but I do not want to be seen as interfering either. I don't want her to feel she is losing face in front of me, or that anything I say would cause her parents to lose face. In our culture this is very important – do not lose face. We would never embarrass Amara or her parents – it is more important to be seen to support her than to risk her losing face if we challenge her reasons for giving up university and if she now regrets these decisions. A very delicate situation, dear.

Also, I should mention Barb has been to the salon for a manicure. We always pretend that we know nothing of Somchai's antics and she acts as if all is well between her and Somchai and also with Amara. She chats away about her life and her job at the TV station. We both know she works in admin in a back office, but she acts as though she runs the station. She then announces that she works so hard she is going to treat herself to a beauty treatment.

"Do you know the Suay Spa?" She asks name dropping a very expensive place in the downtown business district. I know the spa was started by an American lady who has been influenced by new age treatments.

Barb carries on – "I am taking a well-deserved day away from work next week and going there for a number of treatments which I think will enhance my wellbeing."

"I think it will help put a bit of the spark back into my marriage", she says winking.

I nod and smile. If only we were honest with each other!

A couple of days later the Queen of England died. She was 96 years old and respected the world over. What a marvellous woman and one we should all look up to. I hope she is resting in peace now with her beloved husband, Phillip. We did discuss this in the salon, and no-one showed any disrespect or had a bad word to say against her.

Also, this week a rep for a Wellness company came into the salon to ask if I would be interested in stocking their products. Her name was Renata. There were products to appeal to quite a wide audience. There were relaxing night creams, aromatherapy inhalation essence, and a balm that you rubbed into the soles of your feet to help you sleep. There was also a drink that you could buy which was a blend of mushrooms and herbs. I tried one and it tasted just like coffee. According to Renata it should give you a boost. I was impressed with the products and felt that they might sell well to my customers. However, I had to think this through. I didn't want to invest in stock that didn't sell. I would receive a commission each time a product sold, so it would potentially increase my turnover.

I told Renata I would let her know within the next week if I was interested to stock the products.

The following Saturday we closed at 4 pm and I caught the train home. That evening, I had three good Thai friends coming over and I was looking forward to cooking for them. I love cooking for my friends, and I stopped at the international market on the way home to buy food. I always cook several dishes and we share the food. In my country sharing is giving. I am going to make two curries – a red chicken curry and a red fish curry, plus Thai chicken fried rice. I can't wait to get home and start cooking. I just have time before my friends arrive to set the table and change. Anong arrives first carrying a bottle of SangSom and he is followed by Davika and Noi who bring wine and flowers. I can't wait for an evening of friendship and good food….

Recipe for Thai Red Fish Curry

This recipe works with any Thai curry paste and any firm but flaky white fish but this version uses cod and red curry paste.

Ingredients

Fillets of cod, sliced to be about ½ inch in thickness if they are supplied thicker. Enough for 2 people.

1 tbs light oil such as peanut oil

½ a red onion, minced

15 grammes grated ginger

3 cloves garlic, finely minced

1 or 2 tablespoons red Thai curry paste

Tin of coconut milk

2 tablespoons of fish sauce

1 tbs light brown sugar

A handful of fine green beans topped and tailed and diagonally sliced.

Method

Heat the oil in a wide frying pan and add the onion.

Stir over a medium high heat until the onion becomes translucent, then add the garlic and ginger and stir for a couple of minutes, creating a lovely aroma.

Add the coconut milk red curry paste, sugar and fish sauce. Heat until it nearly boils and reduce slightly to a simmer.

When the sauce mixture is heated, maybe try a little taste and adjust the mix slightly.

Add the beans and the fish, allowing the fish to sit in the sauce.

The fish and beans will cook quickly, in a few minutes. Do not stir the pan, but use a spoon to ladle the sauce over the fish. When the fish has turned white, test it by breaking into a piece to check it is cooked.

When you are happy it is cooked, serve with rice.

Ellie - Helps Niall to present his point of view at a meeting

This has been a very busy and, in some ways, illuminating week. It was the week when I first started to believe I should speak up and make sure my voice was heard. I had been living in a comfort bubble for so many years and these new thoughts were something of a revelation to me. However, the week also ended very badly with my confidence shaken, but I am getting ahead of myself...

It all started last Saturday night when Kevin and I and his mother went to watch Niall play with his band "The Brothers of Swing" at the Twisted Oak. Kevin started complaining as we were getting ready to go.

"Why do we have to go?" he complained "Frank Sinatra cover songs – I am sure the place will be full of retirees. Minimum age 80 – on Zimmer frames and doddering about and we will look completely out of place. Also, I can't stand Frank Sinatra or Dean Martin songs. I have the feeling that it is where Niall met mom originally and convinced her to go for dinner with him. She must have looked like a young and fun person in a place like that. What she sees in him I will never know."

I stood up for Niall "They don't just do covers" I said "they write their own songs. They have written enough for an album which they uploaded onto "Music World" and they have had some plays on digital streaming sites."

Kevin laughed out loud "Ellie, anyone can upload music onto "Music World" provided they pay a fee! What I would be interested in is how many sales has it generated? I suspect zero, or a couple dozen from friends. He is hardly living the life of the music mogul, is he? He works full time as a driving instructor and scrounges off my mother".

He ranted on for quite a while. By now I was convinced he was jealous of Niall – both for his good looks and his relationship with Jenni.

I managed to appease Kevin by telling him Jenni was going to treat us to a meal at The Palm restaurant in the downtown afterwards. They do the most delicious filet mignon that Kevin loves.

So we all went to the "Twisted Oak" to hear the band play.

The set "The Brothers of Swing" played was excellent in my opinion. I do like Frank Sinatra even though he is from another era. The band also played a couple of their own numbers, which I really liked. Glancing across the table, I could see Jenni was enjoying every minute. She looked so chic and slim, I felt like a beached whale at the side of her. I had put on a summer dress I have worn a few times previously. I felt it was still flattering, but the problem was every time I wore it – it seemed tighter. I was conscious it was straining a bit around my breasts! Kevin in a blue shirt and chinos sat sulking and had a few beers.

Afterwards in the Palm Niall told us that his presentation was on Friday evening of next week. I had sent him some statistics to put into his presentation and he was going to send me a first draft of his speech for me to review. He had invited a number of local musicians to the presentation, and they seemed keen to come and listen to what he had to say.

Kevin said "I admire you for trying Niall but let's face it you are going into a super competitive business. The streamers and record companies will only pay for what they absolutely have to. It seems to me even if the streamers pay a pittance, they can still find bands willing to let them play their music. I mean are you in a union?"

Niall responded "No we are not – but this is something we need to think about. This is in the speech – you should come and listen to it Kevin"

Kevin responded that he might, but he may be busy on Friday evening.

Overall, it was quite a nice evening, and I enjoyed the steak and cocktails. I knew I needed to diet but figured that tomorrow would be soon enough…

I drove home, as Kevin had had a few beers – he lounged in the passenger seat and ridiculed the idea that Niall could ever make a difference to the music industry. I didn't speak but his attitude annoyed me.

On Sunday Kevin wanted to take our bikes into the lake area to the far north of the city. It was still quite hot and after a couple of hours I was tired and sweating and longing for a nice café where I could have a break. My mind was full of the presentation for next Friday. We finally returned home late afternoon and Kevin went into the den to prepare his classes for Monday. I knew I should be looking at my classes but instead I went into my emails and looked for the copy of Niall's presentation. I read through it. I was impressed how passionate it was about how unfair the system was to musicians. However, in my opinion the speech was not very well put together.

I sat reflecting on this – for so many people music was just a hobby – something they did in addition to their main source of income. People worked in their regular jobs during the day and played gigs in the evening for a few extra dollars. It seemed from reading an article online in the Los Angeles Times that most musicians did not have an equivalent union to SAG-AFTRA they could join until recently. The Union of Musicians and Allied Workers was founded just as the pandemic took hold in 2020. The Union has a vision to help musicians to be paid fairly. They also state on their site that they wish to "reclaim and redistribute resources from the few wealthy companies that dictate the music industry to working class artists and musicians". These are very strong words. The Union aims to build solidarity across gender, race and border. Also, it seems they are concerned about the musicians who are "working" musicians but not necessarily famous and making large sums of money. Ordinary people like Niall and his band "the Brothers of Swing". The Union has various subcommittees that are looking at perceived injustices. It seemed in July of this year, Rep Rashida Tlaib had apparently issued a letter to Congress calling for a new streaming royalty. - she felt that there was no regulation over what should be paid as royalties. Payments per stream were tiny and getting smaller every year. It seemed if Niall could get more "ordinary" people to join this union, then they could work together to try to get better conditions.

Thinking about marketing and the Union I knew I could help by changing the presentation so that it read better and would have a clearer message. Starting to type I slowly went through and changed the message to make it bolder and more forceful. I then emailed it to Niall.

I put the speech to the back of my mind during the following week as I was busy with work and then on the Thursday, I read the news that the Queen of England had died. She was 96 years old and respected the world over. I felt sad reading the news reports but also inspired by her long life and commitment to service. There were some lovely tributes in the papers and on the news.

On Friday evening I went to Niall's presentation. Niall had messaged me to thank me for the amendments to his speech and that he was going to speak from this version.

I went alone as Kevin called off at the last minute saying he was going to the gym.

Niall was speaking at the public basketball pitch in the park in Gent Town. Gent Town is an area in the northern suburbs that is the first stop on the metro outside of downtown. We live a lot further out of the city, also in the northern suburbs, but a few stops on the metro. I was not familiar with Gent Town, but I knew there was a park there with wooded areas and a lake. I imagined it would be a nice place to have the meeting. Also, I had heard on the local radio and in the nail salon that house prices were on the rise in Gent Town – it was becoming gentrified.

I dropped Kevin off at the gym and then drove my car down to Gent Town and the park. I found a parking space not far from the park gates. I could see the basketball pitch was not too far to walk from the gates. As I walked, I felt a bit nervous as it seemed that the park was very run down and there were what seemed to be drug dealers conducting business under the trees. No one spoke to me but I felt I was being watched. There was a children's playground I walked past but no children were playing, instead there were teenagers hanging about on the swings, smoking joints and swearing.

I was relieved when I arrived at the basketball pitch and saw Niall was there. He had set up a table and two chairs and he was intending to speak through a megaphone. When I arrived, there were only a few people there and I wondered if some of the teenagers I had seen in the playground had followed me. I was worried it would be a disaster but by the time he was due to start speaking the area was full of people.

Niall began to speak – and he had memorised the speech, so he had no need to refer to his notes. He was very passionate and as he spoke, he made it clear how difficult it was to earn money as a musician – the poor returns from streamers – if you even got play time. Apple had put the pay up to 1 penny per stream – but it was still very low. Royalties were only paid to the person who wrote the song – even if all the band performed the number. The threat of Artificial Intelligence (AI). The AI threat related to how algorithms could be used to choose songs to play on the streamers. Niall said he understood that another threat was that someone's voice could be used to make a song using AI and these computer generated songs were becoming more convincing as time went on.

He went on to discuss how there was no consistent payment and thus musicians often received a low rate of pay for gigs. He then mentioned the Union of Musicians and Allied Workers and how they were working on behalf of the ordinary (not famous) working-class musician to get better pay and conditions. He urged all present to join the Union and to start to stand up for their rights.

There was a fantastic atmosphere and as he spoke people began to cheer him on. At the end everyone applauded him and then people came over asking how they could join the union and what they could do. So far, it was a really great evening.

After I left the presentation, daylight was fading, and the park seemed more menacing than ever. I now ask myself why oh why didn't I ask Niall if he would walk with me to my car? But he seemed busy and surrounded by people interested to talk to him about signing up for the Union. In fact, I was the first to leave the meeting. Everyone else was talking and hanging around. However, I wanted to leave to pick Kevin up at the gym as I had said I would be there when his class finished at 7 pm.

I set off walking on the path through the park. I had not got far when someone passed me on a bike and stopped in front of me. I moved to one side to get past and then I realised that someone was behind me and the person in front on the bike was blocking the path. They were only young kids, probably in their mid-teens, but they felt so menacing. I was terrified. "Let me pass" I said. "Sure" the one in front of me said and moved closer. A third person turned up now and then a fourth and I realised I was surrounded by teenagers. Where were the people who had been watching the presentation? I could feel myself panicking.

They were closing in. "What do you want?" I said. "Move out of the way and let me pass".

I then saw that the person who had just turned up had a knife. He had it in his right hand and was stroking it with his left hand. He pointed at my purse and indicated handing it over.

I know it seems pathetic, but I opened my purse and handed over my phone and my credit cards.

As I did this, he took hold of my hand and indicated the ring I had inherited. Yes, I gave that to them as well. Then, I ran towards the car shaking and crying. When I was safely inside with the door locked, I managed to calm down enough to drive to the gym. Of course, I couldn't ring Kevin as I had no phone. I kept telling myself I am safe – nobody touched me, it is only possessions. Thank goodness they didn't take my car keys or house keys.

When I arrived at the gym to pick Kevin up and he saw how shook up I was he became very worried, and he wanted to know what had happened. He was really upset. He insisted on driving me home. When we arrived home, he sat me down on the couch and made me a stiff drink. Then he called the police and was told that someone would come out to see us. He shook his head saying he had no idea that Gent Town Park was dangerous.

He then rang his mother to tell her what had happened. Niall was with her as he had gone to visit her after the presentation. They were both upset too. Niall had known the park was a bit dodgy and felt awful leaving me to walk to my car alone. He realised now that he had been thoughtless, but he had been so busy with the presentation…… Jenni also knew about the park and had not been too happy with Niall picking it for his presentation. When he came off the phone Kevin was now furious. " I don't want you helping Niall ever again" he said.

The police then arrived, and I had to go over what happened. Apparently, from what they said muggings and robberies were common in Gent Town Park which had a bad reputation in the city. We seemed to be the only people who did not know about this!!

We had to file a police report and it was so sad reporting the ring stolen. The police asked if we had insured the ring separately. We had been short of money and had not but could still claim on the house insurance.

We then rang to cancel my credit cards. Already there had been some small purchases made at a coffee shop downtown. Then using Kevin's phone we rang to report my phone as stolen.

I was shaken up but not physically harmed so I knew I had to go to work as usual the following week. I used Kevin's phone to contact Janine and Kara by WhatsApp to tell them what had happened. They were horrified.

Lying in bed later that night I relived the moment in the park when I was surrounded, and I started panicking again and I was terrified. It was a long time before I could sleep.... I looked at Kevin snoring away. I knew he loved me and cared for me, but I had felt so alone in the park when the kids surrounded me.

What a week with highs and lows – I had felt so empowered when I was helping Niall with the speech and then so panicked and frightened when surrounded by the kids in the park....

Janine - Training for a 5K

This week I did not have to ring granny to discuss the podcast – she rang me. She could not believe that Meghan Markle had described herself as ugly as a child when she had black frizzy hair and "gappy" teeth.

"What is wrong with black frizzy hair?" granny said. "I like black frizzy hair. Your hair was beautiful Janine when you were a child and still is."

She ranted on for a while. Amy had "gappy" teeth and frizzy hair and she has always been a beautiful woman. And so on...

I wanted to know what happened when granny spoke to the doctor about the possibility of her taking up running. She told me he had been very positive and said that running would help her to keep mobile and supple. It would also help keep her muscles toned. He checked her blood pressure and said it was a bit on the high side and her weight (she was slightly overweight). He recommended that she follow the plan the fitness instructor at the gym suggested to get fit enough to do a 5k`. She said the plan would take her from someone who had never run to someone who could run in a 5k in 9 weeks. The plan was called "Couch to 5k" and was organised by the Running Club. The doctor had also recommended changing her diet to be more healthy by including more fruit and vegetables.

I had my doubts about this – after all granny is in her 70s and has been sedentary for a number of years now. She does get out a couple of times a day to walk Roger, her dog, but certainly nothing more active.

To be honest, I was surprised that she and Amy were working out to Robert John videos. They went to one another's houses every other day and did one of his videos. His videos were walking videos and also had some cardio in them. I knew that running was the next step but wasn't sure if granny and Amy would be able to do it at their respective ages. I felt worried about them and thought it might be better if they took up flower arranging.

Then granny dropped the bombshell. "Why don't you join us, Janine? We start next week. You will have to commit to 3 nights per week where you go out running with a group and then in 9 weeks you can take part in the 5k in the downtown."

Well, what could I say? I didn't want my granny who is 40 years older than me to show me up, so I said, of course, yes I will join you.

On Wednesday I went to have my nails done after work. The salon was full as usual, and Ellie was sitting next to me. She was really passionate about musicians getting paid next to nothing for gigs they performed and by streaming services. She was talking about Niall, her mothers-in-law boyfriend who plays with the "Brothers of Swing" apparently. I had never heard of the band or seen them perform. It was also not something I had thought about before and I found it interesting. I know there are a few artistes that are famous and make a lot of money from their music, but I had not really considered the thousands of others that might be writing their own music but struggling to make money. It seemed from what Ellie said that it was easy to find a distributor for your music but much harder for it get noticed and played sufficiently to make any money. It was shocking the amount of money streaming services paid per play in my opinion. However, I began to think being a musician is rather like being an artist. You have to have a unique selling point. I have found mine working with other artists in a cooperative where we promote African art. We use this promotion to advertise our cooperative and make it stand out from other artists' studios in our city and across America.

"Perhaps Niall needs to think about how he can promote his band and what make it unique?" I said.

"Also who are the fan base for the band? Does he have a database of fans and is he in contact with them?"

Ellie thanked me for these ideas and said she would pass them on to Niall. Apparently, there is a meeting organised where Niall is going to speak and try to encourage others to join a newly formed musicians union.

While I was thinking about how to promote a business, by a coincidence the following day we had a surprise visitor to the Artist's Cooperative. It was Edgar Dumont, the new Mayor of the city. He appeared unannounced with a couple of his colleagues. He said he had been having a walkabout in the downtown area and was interested to find out more about what we were doing. He talked about street art and livening up the city. He had been on a visit to Austin, Texas and he had seen art on buildings across the city. He felt this showed the spirit of the city and its people. He had been to 1st Street and seen a beautiful mural like a postcard that said greetings from Austin. He wondered what we thought about street art. I mentioned the Polka Dot Wall on Montana Ave in Los Angeles and I also commented that I was going to go to Atlanta to the Living Walls Festival. Mayor Dumont was very interested in these projects and said he would be in touch again soon. I wondered if he was planning an art installation for our city?

To be honest I am kind of dreading next week – I can't believe I told granny I would join her and Amy in the "Couch to 5k" training plan! Yet I feel I also can't let her down…

Amara - Too ill to go to the party…

I am still with Dean, and we message every day and meet up regularly. It is something to look forward to after long days in the nail salon making polite conversation. At the nail salon I do find out a lot about people's private affairs though – they seem to like confiding in their manicurist. Take Belinda she lives in a house like ours with her family. She is a salesperson for a pharma firm and has to travel and leave her family some nights during the week. They have a live-in nanny but she feels she is missing so much of her daughters growing up. Then there is Joyce who has given up her career to look after the children full time. She is happy with the time she spends with them but feels she is getting older and left behind with the way technology has evolved in the workplace. I wonder about my own career. Perhaps sales of some sort would be a good choice for me. I had flirted with the idea of real estate. It feels very confusing.

On Friday night when I got home from the salon mom was waiting for me, acting excited.

Mom said: "Keesha is due back tonight for the weekend and they are having a party for her tomorrow. Can you believe we are invited?"

At this point I try not to roll my eyes. Keesha and I grew up playing together and our moms were always friends. Why shouldn't we be invited? She has an acting role now in a TV series that is a soap opera – big deal.

Mom went on to talk about the party. Apparently, the party is going to be held around the pool next door and there will be canapes and drinks.

"I am guessing it will be dressy. I will have to buy something new to wear tomorrow. Your dad is really looking forward to going as well. He likes to brag to his buddies that he knows a celebrity! We might get some pictures. The rule is no pictures, but I am sure we can sneak some!"

Mom was so excited she was almost smirking. She looked me up and down and said "Have you decided what to wear yet?"

I feel like groaning – "no not yet mom" I say " but I'm thinking about it, don't worry"

I escaped as soon as I could. She hadn't asked about my day, due to the fact that she was so excited about Keesha's party.

That evening Dean and I went to "The Albion". It was a really good night, and he bought the drinks. He finally dropped me home about 2 am. To be honest I was still exhausted when I got up the following day for my Saturday in the salon and not in the best mood. I had completed a couple of manicures when suddenly the door opened and in walked my mom, Keesha's mom and finally Keesha. I felt sick! I had to admit Keesha looked good though. She had had a boob job recently and it really suited her. She had straightened her hair and I think she might have had hair extensions but who cares? I had to admit she looked gorgeous.

Of course, these three became the centre of attention in the salon.

Someone asked Keesha "Do you know Meghan Markle? Have you been asked to take part in the podcasts?"

What stupid questions!! However, Keesha was very polite and said she didn't know her and no she wouldn't be taking part in the podcasts.

The conversation got on to beauty and Keesha said how important it was in her life as an actress in a Soap Opera to always look your best. She felt that it was okay to have boob jobs and straighten your hair as she did these things.

My mom was very protective of her making sure that the questions didn't get too personal.

Her visit seemed to go on for ever. By the time she left with her entourage which consisted of my mom and her mom, I felt like my head was splitting. I felt sick for the rest of the day.

I was so relieved when 4 pm arrived and I could leave the nail salon. When I got home mom was busy getting ready for this evening. Dad was sitting in the living room watching a program on wildlife.

I announced: "I'm not feeling well. I'm going to go and lie down on the bed."

Mom seemed concerned about me "What is wrong? Perhaps if you take a couple of pills and lie down you will feel better. The party starts at 7 pm. You should be okay by then."

I went up to my room and drew the drapes and laid down on the bed. Within a few minutes I had fallen asleep. I was woken by mom popping her head round the door asking how I felt. I said not well enough to go.

Mom and dad went without me and I stayed in bed all night. After they had gone, I got up and helped myself to some snacks instead of an evening meal. I got onto my laptop and into a chat room where I talked to people who were investing in cryptocurrency. At 10 pm I messaged Dean and we messaged back and forth for a while. Having him showing how much he loved and cared for me was such an uplift. He was so sweet saying how beautiful he thinks I am and how he loves to touch my skin and hair. I felt needed and warm and fuzzy after reading his messages.

I vaguely heard mom and dad returning from the party, but I quickly switched my light off and pretended to be asleep in case they checked on me.

In the morning I got up about 11 and mom was sitting in the living room.

She asked how I was and if I felt better. For once, she seemed concerned about me. She said Keesha was disappointed that I hadn't gone to the party. There had been rumours on social media that Keesha was in a relationship with Larry Rex, an actor who had the lead in some sort of "woke" drama on Netflix. He is also a male model and currently has a contract with Dior. From his publicity photographs he looks really handsome and he is also very successful. Mom said that the rumours about the relationship were not true and had been put out by Keesha's agent to keep her name in the news. Apparently, Larry had been dating a blonde English girl for a few years. He was also English and lived most of the time in London when he wasn't filming.

"So who is she with?" I asked.

"That is just it" said mom "she doesn't have anybody at the moment. She also feels lonely living in a new city. She works long hours on the set and then goes home to an empty apartment. It is really hard on her. She needs friends at this time."

I immediately felt guilty. Keesha and I had been friends when we were young. I had missed her party and not made any other effort to go and see her.

After lunch I decided to go round to her house to give my apologies. Keesha was just getting ready to go back to the big city for filming next week. I sat on her bed while she put her things together and we chatted. Soon we were laughing and joking just like we always did.

She said "I would invite you over but we work incredibly long hours – perhaps if we get a break one weekend you could come over and see where I live now?"

I promised I would – but deep down I knew I probably wouldn't .... She had moved on now and I was still here, living with mom and dad and doing nails in Aunt Jinni's salon......

Chapter 4

A new mayor and new beginnings....

In September Jerry Levens, on his morning news show on KAVC98 radio announced to commuters that the city had now returned to full prosperity after the Covid pandemic. There was very low unemployment, rising house prices and a fantastic climate. In fact, out of all the Southern cities, in his view, this city was the best. It was a well-guarded secret, and we should keep it that way to stop people moving here from bigger cities and spoiling its small-town charm. He felt that the new Mayor was only adding to the charm and general liveability of this city with his new policies. The new Mayor, Edgar Dumont, who had been elected by a significant majority in July continued to put his own mark on to the city by making good on his campaign promises in the words of Jerry Levens.

Mayor Dumont had some big plans to unveil. Making use of American Rescue Plan funds he has set out a plan to improve the park in Gent Town. He noted that the playground had become run down and tired and he proposed $700,00 to enhance it and make it state of the art. He also proposed $200,000 to refurbish the paths through the park.

This radio broadcast and the Mayor's plans became a big talking point in the salon in the following week....

During September Meghan Markle had delayed the release of her next podcast out of respect for the death of the Queen of England. When the podcast was finally released the topic was about the label of "Dragon Lady", A label applied to Asian ladies which stereotypes them as domineering and strong but also deceitful and sometimes sexually alluring. Apparently, the term comes originally from the female in the comic strip Terry and the Pirates but also from films such as Kill Bill and Austin Powers. Although she grew up in multi-cultural Los Angeles, Meghan said that she was not aware of the stigmas Asian women faced until she was much older.

Jinni – the dragon lady interferes and stands up for a customer...

So I am a dragon lady am I? I must confess I have been listening to the podcasts by the Duchess of Sussex and realising that in the US I can talk about royalty without fear of consequence I am joining in conversations in the salon about them. The latest one discussed stereotypes of Asian people. That we are strong and maybe domineering. Everyone seems to think I am a strong woman – hopefully not too domineering though!

I am still very careful about how much I will discuss. You see dear one of my rules is that we do not have any discussion of racism in the salon. If the conversation starts to veer that way, then all my staff are told to move it into a different direction.

I tell the customers that I am happy to be in America. The US has been good to me – I have a thriving business and feel welcomed in this city. I am not a victim. That is for sure.

Although I love living here, this week I was horrified to find out about the robbery and mugging of the English lady, Ellie, who comes to the salon regularly. Janine and Kara were concerned for her mental wellbeing after this incident.

Imagine how I felt when Jerry Levens broadcast on our local radio what a great place the city is to live in and how that new mayor is going to spend money refurbishing the children's playground in Gent Town Park. Why?? If the park is overrun with muggers and robbers, it is hardly a place you would take children to play is it? Shouldn't he be spending the money on cleaning the park up first. We discussed this in the salon that day and we felt the mayor was not making best use of the Federal funds.

So, I did something I have never done before I rang the local radio station to tell them about Ellie's mugging. I said Jerry Levens should interview her and find out what happened to her before he gives his support to the mayor's new initiative. The Mayor should be cleaning up the park not designing a new playground. How could children play in such an unsafe environment?

Later that day I received a call from the radio station asking for Ellie's contact details. I gave the number we had for her in our records. It turned out that was okay as she had been able to block her old phone, get a new SIM and use her original number.

The radio station said they would contact Ellie and ask if she would be a guest on Jerry Levens show and give her side of what happened to her in the park.

I will be listening to that with interest – I will make sure to have the radio on in the salon.

Also, this week Renata, the agent from the wellness beauty products company came back to see me about stocking her products at the salon. I had been giving this some thought and doing the sums. I would receive a commission depending on how much was sold. It seemed to make sense to me to stock the products. A number of my customers were people who would be interested to buy some of the remedies and products I felt. I could also do promotions on my social media and website for the wellness products. I decided to go ahead and agree terms with Renata and start selling the products next month. We would convert part of the back room into a storage area for wellness products.

I felt happy having made my decision to sell the products and decided to catch an Uber home that evening. I decided to make something healthy tonight so I made a Thai salad. There are a lot of ingredients but it is delicious and good for you. I stopped at the international market to buy the ingredients on my way. While I was buying the ingredients the thought crossed my mind that I might add a little glass of SangSom to go along with the salad. Time to buy another bottle!

So excuse me now I am going to turn on Netflix, look for a good film and eat my salad and sip my drink in peace after another long day at the salon....

Recipe for a salad

Sometimes a salad is the right thing to eat, and a Thai salad is full of good ingredients and a tasty sauce.

Ingredients

Fine rice noodles, half a nest broken up into short pieces and cooked according to the packet instructions. Set aside to cool.

Sauce

1 birds eye chilli, cut open to scrape out the seeds and the internal vein. Use about a quarter of the chilli, or more if you like it hot!

1 fat clove of garlic, minced

1 tbsp fish sauce

1 level dessert spoonful of golden caster sugar

Combine and set aside while you prepare the salad

Salad ingredients:

1 small carrot, grated

Snap peas, sliced diagonally

2 or 3 spring onions, finely sliced

Half of a small cucumber, peeled and with the seeds scraped out, then sliced into thin batons

A small bunch of coriander leaves chopped

A handful of dry roasted peanuts, chopped.

Once all ingredients are prepared, combine and serve immediately.

Ellie becomes stronger and more outspoken..

I couldn't believe it when my new phone rang yesterday afternoon. It was evening and Kevin and I were on our way back from the university after a long day teaching. We were on our way to the gym. It was Libby from KAVC98 radio station. She asked me if I listened to the Jerry Levens show. I said I did and I remembered that this week he had been talking about the mayor's new initiatives for the city. She told me that someone had informed them of the mugging in Gent Town Park and Jerry Levens felt that was very relevant to the mayor's initiatives and the idea that the city was a great place to live. He would like to interview me about my experience in the park on his morning show. Of course, I said yes!! Libby suggested we do it as a phone in. She said that the station would ring me at 8 am to be ready for Jerry to interview as part of his prime-time commuter show.

At the time I did not know that it was Jinni from the nail salon who had recommended me to the radio station. I only found that out later. I was so upset and shook up by what had happened, but I wanted to share my experiences and at the very least to stop it happening to others. I remember Jerry Levens saying on his show that the mayor was going to use American Rescue Plan funds to build a new playground and paths in the park. But who would bring their children to play in a park that was not safe? That evening I sat down and wrote my thoughts down into a short statement.

Kevin was not very happy about me speaking on the radio in case there were any repercussions. He said it might be best if I let it go now and try to move on with life. We had replaced the phone, cancelled the credit cards and claimed on the insurance for the ring. This was true but I asked him what about the emotional impact of what had happened? The fact that now I looked nervously around me as I walked across the campus at the university, for example. Was this something short term, or would I always feel like this, I wondered.

I was waiting by the phone when it rang at 8 am the next morning. Libby introduced herself and said to hold on and then I would be live on air with Jerry.

A couple of minutes, that seemed like hours, passed. Then she said – you are now on-air Ellie.

Jerry said: "I believe I am speaking to Ellie a university lecturer who has something to say about Gent Town park. As we all know Gent Town Park has been in the news this week with the mayor intending to spend nearly a million dollars in improvements there. Hi there Ellie."

I said: "Hi nice to speak to you Jerry."

Jerry said in a fake English accent: "Oh my, jolly nice to speak to you too Ellie. You are not a native of this city. Where are you from?"

I said "Birmingham"

He said "well that can't possibly be Birmingham Alabama with an accent like that."

I laughed and said "You are correct. I am British."

We went back and forth a few times about me being British and my accent and then he asked if I could tell him about what had happened

I told him about going to the park for Niall's presentation to musicians encouraging them to join a Union. When I left the presentation, I was robbed by a group of teenagers on the way back to my car. I also mentioned that there seemed to be a menacing air in the park and there were groups of youths hanging about. I said that it didn't seem to me to be a place where you would want to take a child to play. I had looked up the American Rescue Funds and what they could be spent on.

So I said "would it not be better to spend the funds on education for children in the area to help them better themselves so they would stop hanging about in the park?"

Jerry said he was sorry to hear what had happened to me and he thanked me for coming online and then he went on to say he would be interested to hear what others had to say.

Apparently, the lines were very busy with people ringing in expressing their opinions.

The first I heard was from Nathan Prichard, who said he was principal of the school in Gent Town. He said that the school had real problems with funding and deprivation – the heating system was so old, and the buildings not insulated and the problem was it was too cold in winter and too hot in summer. "We don't want to send the students home" he said, "but it is very hard to concentrate when you are either freezing cold or boiling hot!"

Then a person came on (I now know this was Amy, a friend of Janine's grandma) and spoke up. She said that she was 72 and she had lived in Gent Town for 50 years. During that time the area had been in a decline. Youths hanging around on street corners. Drug dealers hanging out on street corners Max's mini market had been held up twice recently – the second time Max had been threatened with a gun. She said that she would not dare go into the park -not even in the middle of the day as she knew it was where drug dealers did their trade. There was no point spending money on the park until the area was cleaned up and made safe. When pressed she said she couldn't believe that house prices were on the rise – it was still the same dangerous and downtrodden neighbourhood in her view.

And it went on and on with more and more callers stating how they felt about the neighbourhood.

To be honest at the end I could not believe that when I had gone to the park on Sunday I had not known about the problems with Gent Town. How could I have been so naïve?

The next thing that happened was that the local newspaper "*The Pinnacle*" picked up the story and I was featured in the paper. A reporter got in touch through the radio station and asked if I would go to the park and be photographed where the incident happened. By now Kevin was steaming mad.

"This is ridiculous, Ellie" he said. "Just let it go. You do not want to be in the news as a mugging victim. How will this affect your standing with your students? You want to be seen as an academic not as a victim."

Well there he was wrong. I did want to be in the news. I was enjoying the limelight and also the chance to, as I saw it, help others by telling my story.

I agreed to go to the park provided the reporter met me at my car and walked me to the spot where it happened. There was no way I would have gone on my own! The reporter was called Betsy and seemed nice and friendly. There was also a camera man with us called Brad. I felt safe walking into the park with them and no-one approached us.

I had my picture then in the local paper – which was now also available online.

When Kevin saw the online version he was angry – "why, oh why Ellie can't you leave this alone? Just get on with your life and forget about it." He said.

I felt alive for the first time in years. I had spent years working as a lecturer in the UK. I dropped out of the PhD program as I wasn't interested in the research. I was still given a job teaching at a UK university that was a former polytechnic. I got the position based on my master's degree. I taught first year students an Introduction to Business course and a course on Statistics. These were courses that everyone enrolled in a Business degree had to take, and so there were a large number of students enrolled. I taught as part of a team of lecturers. We did one lecture to all the students in a lecture theatre that we shared each week. We also did several tutorials that we taught on our own. These tutorials were all on the same topic. We repeated the same class for different small groups of students. So I might teach the same topic six or seven times to different groups during the week. In addition, these courses never changed – we never updated them or tried to be innovative.

I went to departmental meetings, but I soon found out the managers and senior academics were not really interested in what I had to say. I was not doing research and did not have a profile outside the university. My views were listened to, but they were never followed up on or taken seriously. After a while I gave up trying to make a point, instead I had my phone under the desk and used to look at social media if I got bored.

I had a very good salary for the UK and I liked the colleagues I shared an office with. However, if I am going to honest, I was never going to be progress or be an academic.

Kevin on the other hand did get his PhD and started writing research papers and going to conferences presenting his research. He supervised master's degree students that were writing their dissertations, holding one on one meetings in his office. He was asked to be an expert in his subject and appear on the local TV station and radio station in Birmingham, England.

Nobody asked me to do anything. Kevin received a promotion – I received nothing.

It had got worse since we moved to the USA. I was not happy working as adjunct faculty in the US where I only got paid for the hours I worked and I was commuting between two universities. I felt second rate and as if I did not have a future. But if I wanted to work in Higher Education it seemed that is all that was available to me.

However, I felt alive talking on the radio or helping Niall. I decided that I wanted to share my views online and find out if anyone was interested in listening. I went onto Facebook and found there were public groups you could join for the Radio Station, local communities including Gent Town and the Mayor's office. I joined the community for Gent Town and began to post about the mayor's initiative. Immediately there was a lot of interest and people responded with their own ideas. This set me thinking how I could take this forward. I pondered whether I could take the best five ideas and ask people to vote? Then put the top idea forward to the mayor's office?

As that week ended, I was still feeling shook up after the mugging and losing the ring. However, I felt I was beginning to speak up and my voice was being heard.....

Janine - Takes on couch to 5K

I was really upset when I heard in the nail salon that Ellie had been mugged in the park in Gent Town. I was surprised she had been walking about in the park on her own at dusk as I know it has a bad reputation.

I think it is fantastic that Jinni rang the radio station and Ellie got a chance to do a phone in and talk to Jerry Levens. I couldn't believe it when granny's friend Amy also rang in and talked about Gent Town.

Gene was a bit sceptical – "why doesn't Amy move if she feels like that?" he said "the area has been going downhill for years. She could move in with your granny and they could save on a rent." Always the accountant thinking about money.

This was the week I was due to start the "couch to 5k" training with Amy and granny. Granny had rung me and told me that she and Amy had been to the thrift store and bought exercise gear to wear to the training. She recommended the thrift store in downtown where she said there was a big section dedicated to exercise wear. I decided to pass on this and wear the leggings I wear to the gym with a UOP sweatshirt.

The training was organised by the City Running Club. The course takes place over 9 weeks. Over these weeks you gradually build up the amount of time you can run versus walk. So, after 9 weeks you should be running for 30 minutes. We were told to go to the bridge over the river just outside the city centre for 7 pm on Tuesday evening. The run would take place along a path alongside the river. There were about 6 people from the running club waiting for us who were going to act as coaches, and about 20 people who were taking part in the program.

We were told that we had to take part in three runs every week. This first run would last 25 minutes. I was immediately worried about granny and Amy – could they manage this much activity?

Kathy from the running club was our coach. We set off along the riverbank and walked for 5 minutes. Amy and granny managed this very well. Then we started on the running. 1 minute of running followed by 1 ½ minutes of walking. This pattern was repeated for 20 minutes. After 15 minutes Amy asked if she could have a rest? The coach was nice and understanding and said she should slow down and just keep walking. She shouldn't stop altogether. So, Amy walked the rest of the way and Granny and I did the walking and jogging.

Afterwards we went to a coffee shop for a drink, and I know this is wrong but we all had a slice of cake!!

I can't believe we have to do this three times this week – said Amy

I am not sure I will be able to get out of bed tomorrow – said granny – my knees are seizing up!

But they did come back on Thursday, and we did it again – this time they both managed to do the 20 minutes of running and walking without stopping.

Then we all came back on Saturday morning to do the final of week one.

I was so impressed with them both. I knew the course gradually introduced more running and I hoped next week wouldn't be a lot harder

Amara - Thinking of the future.....

By the end of September, the fact that I had dropped out of school began to really hit home with me. I saw posts from former school friends on social media who were now in their third year at university and seemed happy. My life consisted of going to the nail salon 6 days a week and chatting to the customers.

My relationship with Dean never really took off. At first, he had seemed loving and caring but after a couple of weeks this felt clingy and possessive. He would text me at all hours asking what I was doing and who I was with. I decided to end the relationship. Then I was back on my own.

Kara still came into the salon regularly. She told me about a job fair that was going to be held in the Marriott Hotel in Downtown the following Saturday. She said I might want to go to find out if there were any jobs that I might like to train for. Jinni agreed to give me the afternoon off to go to the fair.

I spent Friday evening putting together a resume. Saturday at lunch time, I left the salon and walked across the downtown to the Marriott. It seemed very busy at the job fair. I had pre-registered so was given a badge and told to go into the main hall. I saw there was a talk on how to train for a career in cyber security. This was due to start in the next 10 minutes. I decided to go to the talk. A side room was set up with chairs and a podium at the front and TV screen. I sat down and a really cute guy came and sat next to me! We started chatting as we waited for the presentation to start and it turned out he lived not far from me in the Southern Hills. His name was Vinny.

The presentation was interesting but there was a lot of studying involved. It seemed there were high paid jobs, but it would take years of study to get there. I didn't know if I wanted to make that type of investment. Vinny and I both agreed it would involve a large investment of time and also money to pay for the courses.

After the talk Vinny and I went for a coffee in the café on the mezzanine level. We were soon laughing and joking. It turned out that Vinny had graduated last summer with a degree from Florida State University in media and communications but had so far been able to find employment. He was living with his parents in Southern Hills and not doing much while looking for work. He really admired me that I was working at the nail salon. He didn't know what he wanted to do. He was quite interested in working in media – perhaps as a reporter on a magazine or newspaper. There was no rush though – his parents were very supportive. His dad, it turned out, worked as a lawyer in the mayor's office. His mother was also a lawyer and worked in a downtown firm. They were away from the house working for long hours so he had the run of the house and he had spent the summer working on his tan by the swimming pool.

We were getting on so well that time flew by and before you knew it the fair was beginning to close. I hadn't been to a single stall or talked to a single employer!! However, here I was with a really cute guy who seemed interested in me.

After the fair we went to "Bermondo" which is a cocktail bar in downtown. After a few Manhattans Vinny ordered an Uber and we staggered outside. I snuggled up to him in the back of the Uber and we kissed. It was beautiful. I could not believe how lucky I was to have met such a gorgeous guy at the job fair.

When I staggered into my house mom was in the family room watching TV. She put the TV on mute when I walked in and started to tell me about her day at an expensive spa. She had had a mud treatment – this had involved (I think) taking pots of spa mud and spreading it all over her body and face. She then relaxed in a steam room for a while. The mud was acting as a detoxifier to her skin. She then washed the mud off and a spa worker applied a scrub to her body. She felt new and refreshed.

She then went on that she needed spa treatments having to put up with dad and his erratic behaviour. She never knew where he was – and right now she needed him here to make us a meal. She hoped if ever I got married it was to someone who treated women well.

She never asked me anything about my day. She just went on and on. As soon as I could I escaped to my room and checked my social media and messages.

An hour later I heard the door open, and dad arrived. Then there was a lot of shouting and swearing. I put in my ear pods and tuned into Spotify.

Eventually mom came up and said a meal was ready – we ate in silence. Dad looked worse for wear again and mom looked angry. Who in their right mind would ever want a marriage like this? I couldn't wait to go back to my room.

Chapter 5

Where the real issues begin to be addressed....

By October Edgar Dumont, the new Mayor, had started to put his mark on the city. He had announced the intended park refurbishment and had gone on to bid for more Federal money to enhance the transportation system linking downtown with the suburbs. However, these were only the first steps in Edgar's plans for the city. Edgar had very big ideas for the refurbishment of the downtown and particularly the socially deprived areas immediately surrounding the downtown. These plans had yet to be announced to anyone outside of his very close circle of colleagues. He had a strategy, and he was sharing this with others very slowly.

Jerry Levens', morning commuter show on KAVC98 radio continued to be popular. Jerry was never afraid to take on controversial subjects, particularly if they related to the city and the wellbeing of its residents. He believed that the new mayor was going to prove controversial, and he was keeping a close eye on the mayor's plans.

"*The Pinnacle*" were also watching and reporting on the mayor's plans – waiting eagerly for each new announcement.

Meanwhile house prices continued to rise in the suburbs and muggings and robberies were also on the increase in the inner-city areas. In a comment to an article about the Mayor in "*The Pinnacle*" the Mayor was described as crazy and out of touch with the ordinary working man. In the inner-city areas, the median income of a family was only $30,000 as compared to $90,000 in the Southern Hills. When was the Mayor going to do anything to help these poor families? Refurbishing the park did not seem to count in the views of Pinnacle readers.

In the walks district of downtown "the Purple Orchid" continued to be very popular and now had started to sell wellbeing products. This was a good business move as customers liked the products and sales went well from day one. It is true to say that at "The Purple Orchid" business was good but on a personal level some dark clouds had started to gather over the owner's life....

In national news the Duchess of Sussex released another podcast "The Decoding of Crazy", In the introduction she said she has been called "crazy" and "hysterical" and ended by saying "opening up about your mental health, it can be really difficult. But if you feel like you need to, we encourage you to do so." On October 11, 2022 writing in the Metro publication online, Jasper King said "Meghan opened up about how she felt suicidal during her time in the Royal Family but she does not reveal in the latest podcast episode who has branded her 'crazy'".

Jinni - Tries to remain calm in times of stress

This week I began to sell well-being products in the salon. I had worked all weekend sorting out the back room and a carpenter I know put shelves up for me on one half of the room. On Monday the products were delivered and stored in the back room. I had a display on reception and for the first week only, I gave away samples to customers who came in for their nail appointments. I also put the products onto my website. From the first day they were popular. It was a good business decision.

Also, this week, everyone wanted to discuss Ellie's spot on the Jerry Levens Show and how the mayor should spend the Federal money. I decided not to share with the customers that I lived in Gent Town for a while when I first moved here. I have to say I didn't like it. I lived in a one bed walk up apartment with paper thin walls and noisy neighbours who used to shout and throw things at one another every night. I had left my husband and moved to this city to be near my brother Somchai. Back then I didn't know that his marriage was arguably much more unhappy than mine had been. As soon as I was settled and had saved enough, I moved further out from the downtown to the northern suburbs where I live now. I would always have a bad opinion of Gent Town and could never see it improving.

The customers were also talking about Meghan Markle's latest podcast about women being labelled as crazy and hysterical. Ellie had something to say about this too. She felt women should be able to manage their emotions in social and business interactions so that they did not appear hysterical. In my opinion, Ellie always provokes arguments. Kara said that she felt it was okay for a woman to show her emotions and that did not make her crazy. They argued back and forth for a while. In the argument they also mentioned that Prince William and his wife Princess Kate had spoken as part of World Mental Health Day on the BBC. This was a special edition of *Newsbeat* about the mental health of young people. I feel it is wrong for a member of a Royal Family to be discussing emotions and mental illness on the radio. This would never happen in my own country, and it is hard for me to understand.

Amara joined in the discussion saying she had a new friend called Vinny who had been talking about Prince Harry. Vinny's mother worked for a company where employees could get wellbeing counselling from a company called BetterUp. Prince Harry was Chief Impact Officer for BetterUp and had spoken up saying that when you are working it is important to put wellbeing and happiness first. If people left jobs that did not bring them joy, this should be celebrated, Prince Harry had said. Vinny said he talks a lot of sense. We all spend a lot of our time at work, and we shouldn't let it affect our mental health. Mental health and happiness should be first. In Vinny's view these are much more important than money.

Ellie asked Amara where Vinny was employed, and Amara indicated that Vinny did not have a job at present. He was taking his time to find a job that brought him happiness and joy. He was living with his parents while he looked for a job. He wasn't going to settle said Amara and she felt that was to be admired.

Kara asked if Vinny's parents worked and what they did. Amara said they were both lawyers.

Kara then said, "I see" and then went on to say that that sort of thinking is fine if you have rich parents that will support you. However, the rest of us have to work to pay the rent or mortgage to buy food and to survive. In fact, she said, in this country many people choose jobs based on healthcare benefits. Many stay just for these which are more valuable than the salary or job satisfaction. It's called survival for the family.

Amara was bristling at this, and I felt that I had to intervene to move the conversation on to safer subjects. I walked over with a couple of my new well-being products which I offered to Kara and Ellie as free promotions and began to talk about the benefits of these products.

I felt Amara needed a break and this week she has taken a couple of days off to go to Florida with her parents. I have grown to rely on Amara and without her it has felt especially busy. She was going with her parents to Florida to visit Barb's cousin Suzanne and her husband Steve. This was to celebrate Steve's special birthday. Steve was going to be 50 years old, and Suzanne was throwing a very big party. Barb had been into the salon on Monday for a manicure and pedicure. She was very talkative and looking forward to meeting her cousin in Florida and going to the party. She went on at length about the party and how much it was costing and how many people were coming to it. I tuned out most of it and thought about what I was going to make for my meal tonight while nodding and smiling and making polite noises. Barb told me that Somchai loves Florida – he had often talked about moving there and living by the ocean. He particularly liked apartments in a marina development not far from Suzanne and Steve. Maybe they would do that when they retired. In the meantime, it was going to be a good family holiday. However, right on cue, as her appointment was ending, she asked how much it would be. She has been so many times she must know the prices off by heart. But she knows I will say "oh for you a 10% discount." What a fool I am – but I love my brother, so I do it.

As she left, I had a bad feeling I just couldn't shake.

That evening I spoke to Arpa in Thailand online and she said she felt Somchai was unhappy in his marriage, and she wished we could do something to help him.

I suppose I was oblivious to what was going on during that week – as I said the salon was especially busy without Amara and each day I was exhausted by closing time.

On the Saturday I closed up the salon as usual at 4pm and as I walked out of the door, I couldn't believe what I saw. It looked like Somchai was waiting outside. At first, I thought it was my eyes deceiving me – it couldn't be him – he was in Florida and due back tomorrow. All sorts of thoughts went through my head – perhaps they had had to come back early? Perhaps someone was ill? I hoped it was nothing serious.

When he finally spoke, I must have looked shocked.

"I didn't go to Florida" he said "I'm leaving Barb and moving in with Randi. We have rented an apartment together".

I looked at him with my mouth open. I didn't know what to say.

He told me he believed that this was a good week to move out. He couldn't stand Suzanne and Steve "showing off" as he put it. He was sick of rich Americans talking about money all the time and making him feel like he had lost face. Also, with Barb and Amara away he could sort things out at the house.

He told me that on the day of the trip he had told Barb that he had been ordered to work this week by his manager. If he didn't go into work, he would lose his job. He had called off going on the holiday. Barb and Amara were very disappointed he was not going but had left in a taxi for the airport. In fact, he had taken vacation days and spent the days they were in Florida moving his clothes and other possessions out of the house he shared with Barb. He had now moved into the new apartment with Randi.

He was going to go and meet Barb and Amara at the airport tomorrow to tell them.

He didn't want me to be mad at him. He loved me and needed my support.

We got into his car and drove back to my place. He wouldn't come in as he said Randi was expecting him at her house.

I said goodbye and went into my apartment. Sitting down with a drink in my hand memories flooded back of the end of my own marriage. I know Somchai was unhappy, but he was now leaving his wife and child for someone else. But I also knew I had aided and abetted him to get together with this woman. Perhaps I am a crazy woman – someone who lives by their emotions. In my mind Somchai is unhappy so I wanted to make him happy by letting him use my apartment for sex with a woman other than his wife. But why couldn't I speak to him about his infidelities in a rational way and encourage him to save his marriage no matter how difficult that would be? I really couldn't answer that question. I knew deep down that was because I didn't like Barb and found her overbearing and bossy. Yet she was the mother of his child, Amara, who I loved.

I am sorry to say I drank all evening until I could hardly walk or talk – sitting in the chair with the tears running down my cheeks.

On Sunday I lay in bed imagining him at the airport as Barb and Amara meet him oblivious to what he is going to say and my heart breaks for them all....

Ellie - becomes increasingly militant....

To be honest with you I haven't been going to the gym much – I have dropped Kevin off there and gone home on the pretext that I would make us a healthy evening meal. Kevin has seemed happy with that arrangement, and I go and pick him up after about an hour.

I do cook while I am at home alone but often it is simple things such as spaghetti and meatballs or a pre-prepared lasagne which I pop into the oven. I then sit and write messages on my iPhone which is more interesting. I will never be a cook I am afraid. I am always on the Gent Town residents' group on Facebook and I am pleased that this has grown in popularity. It is a private group but there are over 10,000 members. Last night I had written that I felt we should take ideas for Federal spending to the mayor. Perhaps there should be a vote for the most popular ideas?

Tonight, I dropped Kevin off and arrived home alone. I put a lasagne in the oven to warm up and tipped a prepared salad into a bowl. I opened a pack of Fritos to snack on while I waited for the food to warm up. I then looked at the Gent Town group and saw I had got over 100 responses to my post from last night. I started to flip through them. I drew in my breath when I read one that said.

"No fat chicks in Gent Town. Fxxk off. We don't want you here"

This response had several likes.

Fat chick?? How rude. How could this person even know what I looked like? Then with a sinking feeling I realised my picture had been in *the Pinnacle*.

I told myself insults like this didn't matter. I thought of the old saying "sticks and stones may break my bones, but words will never hurt me". But the old saying was not true, the comments did hurt. I know I shouldn't be bothered about it, but I was. What was best way to respond to it? Ignore it or respond in a witty put down way? I guess it would have to be ignore as I didn't know how to be witty.

When I picked Kevin up, I told him about it. He did not respond in the way I would have hoped.

"Look Ellie I feel you are playing with fire getting involved with Gent Town politics and Niall's band. You don't live in Gent Town – you live in a nice middle-class suburb which, if you remember, we picked because it is relatively crime free and has tree lined streets. You had a nasty experience in Gent Town

Park. But come on you must put it behind you now. Life moves on. I am always the pragmatist. I believe in practical applications not high-level ideals. Yes, it might be hard to grow up in a neighbourhood like Gent Town but thinking about it practically, it is nothing to do with us. Let the Mayor and the elected officials address the Gent Town problems. Same with Niall's band. Yes, maybe some big companies are making lots of money off the backs of the working class. But again, not our fight – we are not musicians, and we should keep out of it."

I was in the passenger seat of the car and I just sat staring at him, and I suppose he could see that I was upset. So, he softened it and said, "when you have done the citizenship exam Ellie you can vote and have a say in American politics. Until then you should keep well out of these areas if you want my advice."

Well, if I'm being honest, I suppose I didn't want his advice, because I went ahead with the suggestion of a poll for the top 3 things that Gent Town residents would like the mayor to spend Federal funding on.

Many people took part in the poll. Top rated was education and updating and upgrading the local school. This was followed by premium pay for essential workers.

I was happy with the way the poll was going and wondered if I should share it with Jerry Levens who might get even more people to sign up or take it straight to the Mayor's office in an email. I decided to send it to the Mayor's office in an email.

Although I had had a large number of responses to the poll, I also had a few more that were rude about my appearance. These usually said things like "butt out fat chick" or "you should be dieting not lecturing". Although I felt I could rise above this – it still did upset me deep down. When I was in the shower, I was very conscious of my body. I realised that without perhaps making conscious decisions, I had started to change the way I dressed. I now bought elasticated waist trousers and dresses that "flowed". Okay I knew I was overweight, but I didn't really want to face up to it. Surely, I had bigger and better things to do than worry about my weight? Isn't fat shaming a feminist issue? I pondered. Why should I have to starve myself and go to the gym just to appeal to men? Kevin still finds me attractive, I thought. However, a tiny voice inside me said but does he? You don't have sex very often these days, do you? When you come into the bedroom he is usually reading or watching TV. When was the last time you had sex? I knew this was a week last Saturday when we had drunk a whole bottle of wine. I brushed off these negative thoughts. I told myself I am a bigger person (no pun intended) than worrying about my appearance.

On Thursday evening I received an email through my State University account asking me to call by Loni Peterson's office on Friday morning. Loni was the administrator who sorted out the timetable for the part time or adjunct faculty.

I went by her office the following day. She asked me to take a seat and asked how I was. She had read about the mugging in the park in the online "*Pinnacle*" local newspaper and seen my picture.

I said I was fighting back and told her about the Federal funding.

After she had listened, she said she wanted to give me a heads-up. The University was budget cutting and next term they were going to require their permanent faculty to take on more of a teaching load. As a result of this they would be unable to offer me the Statistics course teaching. In other words, they were cutting my hours by a half. She said that she had wanted to give the adjunct faculty the heads up about the budget cutting, so we could look for other work.

I thanked her for telling me and then left her office. I felt sick inside. Money was already tight as it was, and this would make things extremely hard for us. How could the university do this to me? The students had always given me good feedback and the results of my class were good. However, I could be treated in this way because I was only employed on a casual term by term basis. I basically had no rights. I dreaded telling Kevin about this meeting and seeing a couple of my colleagues Ron and Sally sitting in the café I went over to talk to them.

They had also been affected by the budget cutting and were as upset as I was.

Sally was a single mother with two children and did not know how she could support them if her work was going to be cut next term.

Ron, was married but had four children and he was the main breadwinner. This was truly devastating news for him.

Ron asked me if I was a member of the Union? He said that the Union were working to improve the conditions of adjunct faculty, and this budget cutting would be a big setback for the advances the Union had made on this campus.

I was not a member of the Union. I realised I had been worrying about Niall's problems and those of Gent Town – yet I had neglected to protect my own position.

I asked Ron who I should contact to join the Union and he gave me the name and email of the Union rep.

I opened up my laptop and contacted the rep and then got ready to leave. My heart was heavy as I walked out to the car park to meet Kevin and tell him news I knew he would not want to hear.....

Janine - an exciting commission and week two of 'couch to 5k'

At the beginning of the second week of the "couch to 5k" Granny rang to say Amy was getting cold feet. She felt she was an old lady with creaking bones and joints and didn't know if she could do another round of walk/run like last week. Could I try to talk her round?

I ended up ringing Amy and giving her a pep talk. Amy is fiercely independent, and she wants to keep living in her own home. She knows that this is reliant upon her being able to move around and look after herself. After a few minutes she agreed to come to week two of "couch to 5k."

That day at the Artist's Cooperative we had a surprise visitor. It was Ronnie, the Mayor's assistant. She said that she wanted to talk to me about a special commission. The mayor had been so impressed with the way I had talked about Street Art that he wanted me to design and paint a mural on the wall of the new Institute for the Blind and Visually Impaired in downtown. This Institute was due to open in January 2023 and at present the building was being renovated. The outside of the building was to be painted – but the mayor felt a mural would really add to the impact of the Institute in the city. The mural should be something that would celebrate music and art. Obviously, the city would pay me for the mural. I was really pleased to get this commission. It sounded exciting. Ronnie said I should keep them updated as the commission progressed.

I couldn't wait to discuss this with Kara and Ellie. I had some ideas that I wanted to bounce off them. As the Institute was new there were no alumni that I could include in the mural. I felt it should celebrate blind people who were inspiring and had gone on to do great things. I thought a mural of famous blind musicians would be good. Stevie Wonder and Ray Charles came to mind immediately. Kara suggested Andrea Bocelli who is an Italian opera singer. At first, I thought that people might not know who he is, but then I wondered if that might be a good thing? It might get people talking about the mural. Ellie also wondered if we should ask people via the Jerry Levens' early morning commuter radio show who they would like to see on the mural. I thought that was a good idea and Ellie said she would get in touch with his assistant to see if that would be possible.

The following evening, I met with Amy and granny, who were both wearing their new exercise gear, for week two of the "couch to 5k". This week the plan was to start with a brisk 5-minute walk, then alternate 1 ½ minutes of running with 2 minutes of walking for a total of 20 minutes. Our coach from the running club said that we could repeat week 1 if we felt uncomfortable moving on to week two. We all agreed we would try week two and we set off walking along the riverside path.

Granny said it was a bit demoralising as we always ended up at the back of all the other people taking part in the exercise because we walked slower. The pace was supposed to be brisk, but our brisk pace was much slower than the other people. The thing you should know about my granny is that she is very competitive and the thought of being at the back of the pack would really upset her. In her younger days she used to take part in sports and running. She also said that she had kept herself slim and in shape all her life, but some of the younger women who were very large could move a lot faster and she didn't like that! I had to remind her that she was double the age of those women and it was brilliant that she was there.

It was Amy who worried me most as she had never been particularly sporty in her younger years and had sat about quite a bit since retiring. Plus, she liked cooking and eating rich food. She was a little bit overweight and got out of breath easily.

When we started running after a few minutes, Amy panting and wheezing said to the coach: " We are only supposed to run for 1 ½ minutes has your watch stopped?"

But I must give the pair of them credit they managed to do the whole 20 minutes. We finished at the same time as the other runners, but we had not covered as much ground. I wondered if that would cause a problem in later weeks as we were supposed to run a 5k at the end of the training?

We did it all again twice that week – the third time we did it we covered more ground.

Amy calls our coach "The Torturer" and says every part of her body aches but she is up for continuing next week.

I am beginning to believe that granny and Amy will run a 5k one day!

Amara - visiting family in Florida and a sad homecoming...

We went to Miami this week to visit Auntie Suzanne and Uncle Steve. It was Uncle Steve's 50th birthday and Auntie Suzanne was throwing a big party for him. Dad was supposed to come but right at the last minute he called off saying his manager had insisted that he work this week. Mom was furious but he was not to be talked around saying he would lose his job if he didn't work.

We went in a taxi to the airport and had a cocktail in the bar before boarding the plane. I messaged Vinny from the bar. We are close now and I confide in him daily. He was going out biking today and we agreed to talk later.

We were flying on a budget airline, so we had to pay for everything on the plane. We ordered drinks as soon as we were in the air. The steward was so cute though. He had a lovely smile and wanted to chat. Mom was very happy with all the attention he paid me.

"Men like you Amara" she said "you still could be an actress or a model you know. There is still time…"

Oh my goodness!! yawn!! Her voice droned on. I didn't listen and put my earpods in after a while and started listening to Spotify tunes. I saw Meghan Markle had a new podcast, but I preferred to listen to music. Ellie had told me about "The Brothers of Swing" and I looked for them and found them and listened for a couple of minutes to their music. Not bad if you happened to be about 90 years old, I thought.

Auntie Suzanne was waiting for us at the airport in Miami. She always looks good. Today she is wearing Lululemon active wear, and she said she had been to the gym earlier. Mom had to explain what had happened why dad couldn't come. I think Auntie Suzanne is becoming used to dad flaking out at the last minute. She didn't really comment.

Auntie Suzanne and Uncle Steve have a beautiful home and I love staying there. It always feels comfortable and welcoming. I am not sure what Uncle Steve does. I think it something to do with investment banking. I know they are rich by the size of their home and the cars they drive. It is obvious they have more money than we do. Mom doesn't like this, but she does like going to parties and meeting people with money. As a result, she would always come to an event they were organising.

That evening when Uncle Steve returned from work, we had an informal dinner out by the pool. Auntie Suzanne urged Uncle Steve to tell us about his special birthday present. Uncle Steve told us that they had splurged on a Ferrrari car. I thought mom's eyes were going to pop out of her head.

Auntie Suzanne explained that when you buy a Ferrari it is built specially for you. They had been to the factory in Italy and spoken to the designers. This was a weekend visit which had included an informal meal with other people who were buying cars.

"Were there any celebrities?" mom asked. Auntie Suzanne said there weren't so far as she knew. She explained that they were rich people who she believed worked in banking like Steve or were executives in other industries who they got chatting to at the meal.

Apparently, they were told at the factory, that Ferrari only sell their cars to people who they believe will look after them. They might turn you down after meeting you, if they don't think you will take care of the car. It sounded like BS to me, but I couldn't wait to see the car. It was in the garage and really was very beautiful. Uncle Steve offered to take me for a drive in it. We went down the intracoastal highway and it was fabulous!! I want a Ferrari, so that is going to be my aim now.

The party was nice but a bit boring. Most people were old and friends of my Auntie and Uncle. I enjoyed the food and drink and sat by the pool messaging Vinny. I couldn't wait to meet up again.

When we got on the plane to go home and had found our seats, mom started holding forth again and guess what? It was back to her favourite subject – Keesha.

"I'll bet Keesha gets a Ferrari next. She is making so much money as an actress".

"How do you know?" I said.

"Honestly Amara you are so naïve. Someone famous and on a prime-time soap will be rich believe you me. Do you know she got asked to take part in an advert for cryptocurrency last week? That is going to pay a lot of money. You do know that the youngest billionaire in the US made his money from cryptocurrency. He is not that much older than you and already a billionaire".

I could feel myself tuning out – I wonder if there is something wrong with me. My mind can't concentrate when mom is talking. I put my earpods in and ignored her for the rest of the journey home.

Dad was waiting for us at the airport. He seemed vaguely interested to hear about the party and the new Ferrari on the way back home. He made us a meal when we got in and we sat and ate it. Conversation was a bit stilted, but then it always is with my parents.

At the end of the meal, dad stood up and said he had an announcement to make. We both looked at him expectantly.

"This is the last meal I will share with you in this house" he announced.

Mom rolled her eyes "Isn't that a bit dramatic, Somchai?" she asked, "what do you mean the last meal?"

"I am not going to live here anymore. I have met a person who makes me happy, and I want to be with her full time. I am leaving now to go to an apartment where I will be living with her".

I thought my eyes were going to pop out of my head!

"Dad, have you been drinking?" I asked, "you can't be serious".

"I am very serious" dad said "that is what I am going to do. I still love you both, but I can't go on living here. The constant arguments are getting me down. I will keep in touch, but I am going tonight".

He then turned around and walked out of the house!

We sat there speechless for a minute and then mom went upstairs, and I followed. She opened the door to his wardrobe and we saw that it was completely empty and then she opened his drawers and they were the same. Everything he owned had gone, including the TV in the bedroom.

"He hasn't been working at all, has he?" mom said, "he has been spent the whole time we were away getting his things together and moving out."

She then collapsed on the bed and began crying.

I stood there not knowing what to do. I turned around and went to my own room slamming the door. I felt sick to my stomach. I had caused trouble dropping out of UCLA and returning home. I wondered if this my fault? Things had been toxic since I came home from LA.......

I messaged Vinny who said he would come round for me, and we could go for a drink. We ended up downtown drinking in "Vesuvius" a trendy bar. When we got back about 2 a.m. I was decidedly worse for wear and had forgotten dad had left until I saw his car was missing from the drive and the memory flooded back.....

Chapter 6

The Rise of the Bimbo...

The following week there were storms and heavy rain across the whole state. Traffic slowed almost to a standstill on the freeway into and out of the city. There was some flooding on the campus of Gent Town High School and the school had to close for a day until this was sorted. This was reported in *the Pinnacle* and there were more calls for funding for the school to upgrade its buildings and campus. This was also mentioned on Jerry Leven's commuter radio show. People were very interested to find out what the new Mayor had planned for the city. He had stated he had a strategy. When would people be able to find out about this?

The Purple Orchid has advertised a fall special on the local radio station. This consisted of gel nails for a heavily discounted price when a customer also bought wellness products up to the value of 20 dollars. This promotion went well and the salon continued to be busy.

The Union of Musicians and Allied Workers was actively working to improve musicians' rights. On their website they stated:

"We believe that the only way to transform music is to collectively take resources and power from the few wealthy companies that dictate our industry……Music workers are workers, and it is time to get organised and join the fight."

However, nothing had changed and still musicians continued to be paid cents per play on streaming services such as Spotify.

The Duchess of Sussex continued to release a weekly podcast on Spotify. This week her podcast was called "Breaking Down the Bimbo" with Paris Hilton. This podcast proved to be controversial as the Duchess discussed her time as a briefcase-opening assistant on the TV show "Deal or No Deal" where she was objectified for her beauty and not her brains. She felt she was made to be "all looks and little substance" on the show. However, she always knew that she was "so much more than what was being objectified on the stage". She said she did not like being objectified and reduced to a bimbo. In another TV program, Whoopi Goldberg commented "When you're a performer, you take the gig" which sometimes involves a "Bozo suit" or a "big nose" because that's the way it is in Hollywood". She cautioned the Duchess about not making "the other woman feel bad, because they're trying to make a living, too."

Jinni - business success and family troubles...

I went into the salon early on Monday mulling over whether I should ring Barb to see how she was. When Amara arrived for work, I knew it wasn't good. I took Amara into the back room and asked how she was. She told me that Somchai had left the previous night. Barb was distraught. She had gone to work this morning but seemed to be in a fragile mental state. Amara said she blamed herself for causing upset at home with her troubles in LA. I told her not to be so silly. She was not to blame. This was between her parents. Amara did not cry, and we walked out into the main salon with smiles for the customers.

At 6.45 that evening Barb arrived, ostensibly to pick Amara up and take her home. I knew she wanted to speak to me. She looked pale and stressed. She asked if we could speak privately in the back room. I said we could talk when I had finished my last customer of the day. After I had finished the manicure, I was working on, I went into the back room with Barb. She didn't waste any time on pleasantries. She got straight into it.

"Where is he and who is he with?" she asked, "I know you know. He always has to have a little bimbo on the side and this time she has been crazy enough to let him live with her. I know he won't be on his own" She paused for breath "he doesn't earn enough to live on his own. So there has to be a bimbo".

I tried to calm her down, but this wouldn't work. "Come on Jinni" she said "you know who he is with. He confides in you. Tell me"

Finally, I said I knew who he was with, but not where they were living. This was true.

"A hostess from the Black Cat?" Barb spat it out. "Great. Aren't they all brainless blondes? Cheap little sluts. What would he want with a stupid woman? He had a beautiful home and money, and he throws it all away on some bimbo."

She left in a temper with Amara in tow. She never once considered if she had had any part in the marriage breakup – it was all Somchai's fault.

I thought it was best that I didn't know Randi and Somchai's new address then I would never be tempted to give it to Barb. I hoped Somchai was happy with Randi and that he would not regret leaving. Looking at Barb storming out of the salon, it was hard to imagine why he would have wanted to stay.

As I rode the metro home I reflected on how well the salon was doing financially. Maybe I could afford to move to a bigger apartment soon. However, I was aware of the upset and trouble in Somchai's and his family's life. I sent Somchai a text "How are you?" he came back immediately. Randi was not working as it was Monday evening and they were cooking a meal together. When they had eaten, he would ring me.

Later that evening when I was settling down on the couch with a drink Somchai rang. He was happy he said. Randi made him happy. He would come over to see me later in the week when she was on one of her shifts at the Black Cat. "Please don't tell Barb where I am" he pleaded. Then he mentioned that the move had been very expensive, and he wondered if I could make him a small loan just to tide him over until he got back on his feet again after moving.

I know I should never pander to him – cover up for him, lie for him, lend him money. I was a fool. But I knew I would. I loved him and he was my only brother. We were two people from the same family in a foreign country. I had to help him when he needed help.

"How much?" I said...

Ellie - gets serious...

After finding out my hours were going to be cut, I had messaged the Union and asked to join and then I knew I had to tell Kevin. I was dreading telling him as I knew he would be very upset.

In many ways this move to the USA had not gone as planned. We had moved primarily to be near Kevin's mother, Jenni, who we saw as a lonely, old, grieving widow who needed family near her to help her. In fact, once we got here and got to know how she lived her life the opposite was true Jenni had reinvented herself after her husband died and was now a beautiful, vibrant woman in her later years. Additionally, she was not lonely, she had lots of friends and she was a member of the tennis club and an active contributor to charities. And we can't forget the handsome younger man friend Niall. In fact, to be honest, she had a better life than I, as a much younger woman, had.

Since the move we had been struggling financially due to higher housing costs in the USA and my working on short term contracts in higher education.

Kevin looked devastated when I told him about my hours being cut. We were in the car driving home. "Is there nothing else they can offer you?" he said, "perhaps some tutoring at a lower rate?"

I told him that it seemed there was no extra work at the State University with the budget cuts.

"We can't manage financially" he said, "we are just about breaking even each month as it is If you don't find anything else in the new year, we are up shit creek without a paddle."

I mentioned that in the short term we have claimed for the ring that was stolen on our house insurance. We could use that money to help us until I could find other work.

Kevin looked really concerned – "but it was your aunts ring" he said "and had sentimental value. I wanted you to replace it with another ring."

It was difficult – I knew he was right, but we had very little savings. We had put all the money we got from our house in England as a deposit on the house here and we had used most of our savings to make the move over here.

Kevin said he was going to ask his mom for a short-term loan to help us in the new year if I didn't find work.

I then told him I planned to join the Union. Kevin was not pleased with this.

"The Union have been threatening a strike" he said "and this would be devastating for the University. A strike could really affect student satisfaction and recruitment. That is the last thing we want. The university has been coming up in the rankings and, as you know, that is important. I think you should forget the Union. The less support they have – the better."

He also told me that it was not all bad news today as he had heard back from a national research agency that they would provide funding for the research he was going to carry out with Dr John Strickham from Georgia State University. I was pleased for him and congratulated him. Personally, I thought John Strickham was a pumped up arrogant little nerd. We had visited him in Atlanta. Kevin and John had made a presentation on their proposed research at the University. We ate lunch in a restaurant near to the university afterwards.

During lunch John held forth the whole time about his brilliant PhD from Yale, his post doctorate from Oxford and all his publications. Funnily enough John told us that he did not have a partner at present. He brought his research assistant to lunch instead. She sat there hanging on every word "the two great men" spoke and called them both Dr at lunch. "Can I pass the bread to you Dr John" and then "Dr Kevin, would you like some more wine?" . At one stage I went to the toilet just to look into the mirror to check that I wasn't invisible.

I am also sorry to say that the advice about the Union was another piece of advice Kevin gave me that I ignored. When we got home, I checked my emails and saw I had a message from Karl who said he was the Union Rep. The Union was the Adjunct Faculty Union (AFU) He asked if we could have a Zoom conversation to discuss my joining the Union and we agreed a time.

I had also promised Janine that I would contact Libby from KAVC98 radio about the mural at the Blind and Visually Impaired Institute. I messaged her the following day, and she got back in touch with me. She had spoken to Jerry Levens and they both agreed that it would make a good topic for the morning commuter show – especially as it concerned the Mayor and linked back to the earlier discussions about how he was spending money in the city. I gave her Janine's contact details and she said she would be in touch with Janine.

The day after I had my Zoom conversation with Karl who was our local rep from the AFU. He explained how to pay my dues and become a paid-up member of the Union. He then asked about my meeting with the Administrator. I told him about my hours being cut next term. This had happened without any negotiation. He was aware that the University was budget cutting and that other people had been similarly affected. He also discussed the rate per hour that we were paid as adjunct faculty – this started at the equivalent of $24,000 a year. He knew that in most cities that was insufficient for a person to live on. The Union were having a meeting the following week as they were considering taking these points forward to management. I was invited to the meeting which would be on campus. There would be an opportunity to speak up. I made the decision that whatever happened during the next week I was going to go this meeting.

That week Jenni asked us to go over for Sunday lunch. Kevin was still angry about the mugging and robbery after I helped Niall with the presentation. However, we agreed to go. Niall was there when we arrived, and he asked how I was. He was really concerned about me and what had happened the evening of the presentation. We began to talk about the Union of Musicians and Allied Workers that Niall had joined. It seemed they were actively lobbying on behalf of the "working class" musician trying to get more fair deals. Niall had joined their messaging platform Slack and was following their lobbying and had become involved trying to recruit new members. He was particularly interested in their campaign for "Justice at Spotify".

Niall had also talked to other members of "the Brothers of Swing" and they had agreed to record a CD. He said he knew popular opinion is that CDs are old fashioned now but people still buy them. After a concert they had sold a few CDs to fans who were happy to pay $10. This certainly beat revenue from streaming which was $0.003 per stream. Jenni had been with him to a concert and stood on the door selling CDs. She had sold 500 CDs. It was not much, but a start.

I received an answer to my email to the Mayor's office. It was very polite. They thanked me for my interest in Gent Town and for sending the results of the poll. They also said that the Mayor had a strategy to revitalise and energise the City and he would be unveiling that in the next couple of weeks. It was recommended that I follow the news outlets to read about the strategy.

It seemed that things were moving on with my activism. I was pleased that Niall was taking positive action to try to earn more money from his music. I was also determined that I would stand up for my rights at the University. I would go to the Union meeting next week and make sure that my voice was heard….

Janine - planning the mural......

When Libby from Jerry Leven's show rang me to ask if I would take part in a phone-in about the mural at the Blind and Visually Impaired Institute I was really pleased to take part. I thought it was a great idea of Ellie's to ask people during a phone-in what they would like the mural to represent. We agreed that we would do the phone-in on Tuesday morning.

I really enjoyed my time on the show talking to Jerry Levens. Jerry soon put me at my ease and was funny and welcoming. I said that as the Institute was new there were no alumni to feature. We should celebrate American blind people who we felt could act as an inspiration to others. I carried on saying that I had the idea originally of including blind musicians on the mural. But I was interested to hear ideas from other people. The Institute was new and the idea of Street Art in the city was also new, so we wanted it to make an impact and look great. He then opened the lines so that people could ring in with ideas for the mural. There was a very good response.

The first caller said why does it have to be blind musicians? After all Helen Keller is the most famous blind person ever. She was a deaf-blind activist who was also an author and lecturer. An amazing person.

The second caller agreed Helen Keller was very famous but felt a mural of musicians would be very inspiring. Art Tatum was suggested as the one of the greatest American jazz pianists ever.

The third caller said they agreed a blind musician would be good. But how about someone from the south of the USA? Was there anyone from this city?

Jerry and I could not think of anyone. Ronnie Millsaps was from N Carolina and Ray Charles was from the Southern States.

The third caller said that Art Tatum was a great musician but as he died in the 1950s, he might not be recognisable by young people. Also, Ronnie Millsaps and Ray Charles. Why not have someone contemporary? What about Matthew Whitaker?

Jerry said he had not heard of Matthew Whitaker and asked who is he?

The caller said he is a 21-year-old who has been blind from birth. He is a jazz pianist who at 10 years old was the opening performer for Stevie Wonder's induction into the Apollo Theatre's Hall of Fame.

I started to feel excited – maybe on the mural I could paint Stevie and Matthew both playing grand pianos. Neither had links to this city but Stevie was very famous, and Matthew was a young person just starting out on his career. Maybe not all people would know a young jazz musician but as I had reasoned earlier this was not necessarily a bad thing as they might question who he was and show interest in the mural.

When I got back to the studio, I began to sketch it out. Once I had a sketch I was going to meet with the principal of the Insitute and her deputy to show them the sketch and to check they were happy with the idea for the mural.

That evening I was due to meet Granny and Amy on week three of the Couch to 5k run. They had both completed two weeks – although Amy referred to our coach from the running club as "the torturer". This week we met on the riverbank and Barry who was one of the coaches gave a pep talk to the older people taking part. Barry pointed out some of the health benefits of running. It helps blood flow around the body and by building up cardiovascular fitness adds strength to hearts, lungs and blood carrying systems. The less we move the worse our mental health can get. Moving around can affect the "happy chemicals" in our body. He said perspective is important and the way you talk to yourself. Instead of saying "oh I must go running today" – start your day with "I get to go running today".

Barry finished by pointing out that the more exercise we do, the better our mood and the better our bodies feel AND you are never too old to run. If you have arthritis, he said then you might feel stiff in the morning – so this is why we run in the evening. Running might help your arthritis.

I'm not sure if this pep talk really convinced Granny and Amy but they set off and we all completed week three. So far so good……

Amara - finding out the truth…

This week has been one of the most truly awful weeks of my entire life. Yes, it was terrible when I dropped out of UCLA and mom and dad came to pick me up and drove me home. But this week beat that one, hands down.

On Monday evening mom came storming into the nail salon to confront Jinni about dad. She didn't find out much. Jinni told mom who dad is living with, but I am sure she also knows where dad is living. She did not disclose his address. I think she aids and abets dad. As we drove back home, mom said that Jinni was covering up for dad. "Thai people are so under hand and sneaky" she said "it is all about saving face in front of others. Nobody tells the truth. Anything to keep face".

Mom went to work all week, but when she got home, she stomped upstairs to her room and locked the door, and I could hear her on the phone to various people shouting and bad mouthing dad.

There was no food! Of course, dad used to do all the cooking and mom, either doesn't know how to cook, or has forgotten. I borrowed mom's car and went down to McDonalds for food on Monday, Taco Bell on Tuesday, KFC on Wednesday and then back to McDonalds on Thursday. At this rate I would look like a beached whale within a month. Mom moaned she didn't want any of the food when I asked her, and then I heard her get in her car later and I bet she went to the same food outlets!!

Luckily Vinny took me out on Friday for a meal at the Palm, in downtown. What a treat! I had a rare New York strip steak with a salad and a Manhattan. "Oooh food orgasm" I moaned as I bit into the steak and giggled. Vinny laughed and moved his leg next to mine under the table. Later, I smuggled him into my room. Mom was wailing and moaning to someone on the phone in her room oblivious to us. Well, I guess that was a lovely end to my week – the one highlight in a miserable week.

Vinny left before mom got up on Saturday. When she came downstairs, I was sitting at the kitchen island drinking coffee. I asked her if she wanted coffee.

She looked pale and serious "We have to talk, Amara" she said.

I nodded and she sat down next to me.

"Your disgusting father has run off with his little slut and bimbo and left us in the lurch" she said. "And what type of person is she? To break up a happy marriage and take off with the husband. She must have no morals".

She droned on in this way for a few minutes. Then she dropped the bombshell.

"You see Amara I relied on your father's income to run this house….."

Pardon? Are my ears deceiving me? Dad's income?

I looked at her and said "I thought you used grandad's inheritance to buy this house? Also, you work, and you said you earned a lot more than dad. His money was just pocket money".

She went really red in the face "I never said that Amara you do make things up. I have always been very supportive of your father in his career".

"Career? I thought dad worked at the DIY store delivering large orders for customers. You said he earned next to nothing doing it and you said that without grandad's money, if we had to rely on dad we would have had to live in Gent Town."

"Stop making things up Amara. I never said that. You do have an active imagination. The truth is I used all my inheritance to buy this house. I need money from salaries and wages to buy food and for the upkeep of the house, the cars and everything else."

"You bought the biggest show-off house that grandad's money would buy, didn't you mom?" I said "OMG are you saying we can't afford to keep it up without dad's wage?"

"That is exactly what I am saying" she said "welcome to the real world. I have given you a break on your wages at the nail salon. But if you want to stay here, I am going to have to ask for a bigger contribution. Even if you do pay more we might still have to rent a room out."

"Take in a lodger?" I said "Oh mom please"

"Well that is the way it is" she said "now you know what an absolute bastard your dad is"

Could it even get any worse?...............

Chapter 7

The Mayor shares his strategy....

In the fall, due to the popularity of Jerry Leven's commuter radio show and articles in *the Pinnacle,* the online local newspaper, there was a lot of discussion and gossip in the City about what the Mayor's strategy for changing the City was going to be.

The customers in the Purple Orchid were keen to join in the discussion.

Finally, the new mayor, Edgar Dumont, made a guest appearance on the Jerry Leven's show to unveil his strategy. This included a plan to revitalise and energise the area just north of downtown including Gent Town. At present, although the area had a park and some beautiful old homes it was run-down and, in the views of many, dangerous. It was mainly characterised by a 4-lane highway that took traffic out of the downtown to the suburbs. The beautiful old houses had fallen into rack and ruin, businesses were boarded up and vacant and homeless people were sleeping in the doorways. Mayor Dumont explained he had visited Lancaster, California, where they had had problems with people speeding through an area and not stopping and as a result the area had gone into a decline. They had changed the road from four lanes of fast traffic to two lanes of slow traffic passing under palm trees along pedestrian friendly streets. Lancaster had been inspired, he had been told, by the Ramblas of Barcelona in Spain. The Ramblas is a very famous pedestrian walkway through the downtown area of Barcelona. Edgar explained he was working with planners to do something similar with the highway out of the city centre. He felt that would attract shops and cafes to set up in the area. He had already attracted a Blind Institute to take over one of the vacant buildings. He mentioned the mural that was to be painted onto the wall of the new Institute and if that went well, he would be commissioning more street art for the area. He explained that just out of downtown, in Gent Town, the road ran alongside the park and the money he would be spending on the park would change it into a green and beautiful destination for people to visit after walking along the main boulevard.

The lines were jammed after he had unveiled his strategy with people ringing in to share their views. It was a very divisive strategy – with some believing it would revitalise the area north of downtown while others felt the money could be better spend on schools and the police.

These discussions spilled over into the Purple Orchid where people were mainly against the new mayor's strategy. The idea that the new road plan would slow people down was dismissed as not being workable in this City despite evidence that it worked in California.

At this time, the Duchess of Sussex continued to release her podcasts on Spotify. She continued to focus on labels that she feels try to hold women back. She discussed the myth of the angry black woman who is overly emotional. The Daily Mail reported that she felt this stereotype sometimes made her frustrated as she felt she had to cower and "tiptoe into a room" as she was frightened she would be seen negatively. This went against her beliefs:

"I'm particular, I think a high tide raises all ships, we're all going to succeed so let's make sure it's really great because it's a shared success for everybody"

She felt that women should be able to be direct without being called angry.

She also released a podcast on good wife/bad wife, good mom/bad mom. In this episode Meghan opened up about her feelings around being a mom to her two children. The Daily Express reported how in the podcast she explained how she makes breakfast for Harry and the two children and how important this is to her

"I love doing it….and it just to me feels like the greatest way to start the morning."

These podcasts were extensively reported on in the British media and always caused some discussion in the salon…

Jinni - Thinks big…

I had started listening to Jerry Leven's show when I first arrived at the salon in the morning. The show was aimed at commuters, but I felt people who came in early enjoyed listening. After his show, I switched the station to a mellow music station which acted as background and was not intrusive at all.

When the Mayor unveiled his new strategy on the morning show, it caused a lot of discussion in the salon. There were a lot of negativities and I needed to get my own thoughts straight.

To me, the new strategy meant opportunity. If a previous rundown area was going to be beautified and people encouraged to slow down and enjoy the area, then it could represent a huge opportunity for me. I could expand my business, either as a nail salon or I could start a spa offering treatments and selling products. If I did this then this area would be good, I felt. If the area was being redeveloped there could be good deals on leasing properties – these properties might be currently vacant and the fact that the new leaseholder had to renovate the property might be reflected in the lease price.

I felt quite excited thinking about it. I would have to get a loan to expand, but why not? The Purple Orchid was doing very well and was making a good profit. What a great time to expand. I made a mental note to contact my financial adviser to discuss.

It was a couple of weeks now since Somchai had left Barb and Amara to live with his new love, Randi. I still felt guilt at the role I felt I had played in this, such as allowing them to meet in my apartment and hiding the affair from Barb and Amara. Amara seemed upset but behaved professionally in the salon, chatting to the customers as usual. I felt that I should speak to her and check she was okay. It was very difficult though. We are not close. She was polite when I brought the subject up of Somchai leaving and asked how she and Barb were. However, she chose not to confide in me, and I don't blame her.

In fact, I had been in contact with Somchai. I had received a message from him asking me to go over and have a meal with him and Randi at the apartment they had rented together, on Wednesday after work. I had been determined not to find out their address so I would never be tempted to give it to Barb, but I had not seen Barb since that evening when she stormed into the salon. I wanted to know that my brother was safe and had a nice place to live. I felt it would be okay to visit them, so I asked for the address of the apartment they had rented together.

Somchai gave me the address – I saw it was in an area north of downtown on the borders of Gent Town. This area would be included in the Mayor's redevelopment plans. On Wednesday I booked and paid for an Uber out to their new apartment. I could see as the Uber drove from the salon in downtown to the apartment that the area was rundown. It seemed to me that it would require much work and funding to bring it up to a point where people would want to stop here and walk around. At the corner of the street where Somchai now lived there were some old cars parked and what looked like homeless people hanging around. What a change from the big house in Southern Hills where Somchai lived with Barb.

I got out of the Uber and walked over to their apartment. It was in a block of six that looked very tired. The paint was peeling off and the steps up to the front stoop were broken and dirty. I pushed open the front door and walked up to the first floor where their apartment was located. The building had a faint smell that brought back memories of being poor when I had first left my husband and moved to this city.

I knocked on the door and Somchai answered. He was smiling and hugged me. Randi came over laughing and smiling and hugged me as well. Inside the apartment was very small, but clean and tidy and a good smell was coming from the kitchen. Somchai seemed more relaxed and happier than I had seen him for years.

Randi was like a quieter more affectionate version of Barb I decided. As I noted when I saw her at my apartment she is an older white woman who has what I believe is called a "hard face" and dyed blonde hair. She made me feel welcome and at home. We ate a simple Thai green chicken curry and rice. She told me she had never had Thai food before meeting Somchai but was now "hooked" on it. She asked me some questions about the salon and I asked her about her job at the Black Cat. She said she tended bar. I believed her as she really didn't look right to be a hostess.

Looking back, it never occurred to me that it was strange she was not tending bar at the Black Cat and seemed to have a lot of free time. I suppose I assumed that her shift pattern was her concern.

We had a nice evening and I booked an Uber for 11 pm. Somchai walked out with me. "This is a new beginning" he told me "With Randi's help I am going to give up the booze and life is going to be good".

As he waved good-bye, I wished I could believe him....

Ellie - forgets about being a good wife....

I was pleased when the Mayor unveiled his plans for the city on the Jerry Leven's show. It didn't seem that he had listened to our requests regarding the school, but certainly he had plans to turn around a very run down part of the City. Perhaps after the initial work was done, more people would move into the area who would help to lobby for improvements to the school etc.

I was still writing on the Facebook group for Gent Town and had also taken to other forms of social media to get my message across about how dangerous the park was. I had also written an email to *the Pinnacle* which had been published in the paper. I always received many responses to my messages. However, I had now received more cruel responses to my messages – usually from people writing under a pseudonym. I was called fat by these people and told to keep my nose out of things that didn't concern me. Being called fat was hurtful but it was the way these comments were written that was particularly bad. The use of profanities and saying that they couldn't imagine any man wanting me. People saying, I was so fat that perhaps I had nothing better to do and that is why I wrote on these pages? Wicked remarks. There were also threats to my safety if I went back to the park. I could not believe that Facebook allowed this. When I checked into it, it seems they did not allow it, and I could report these messages as being against Community Standards. When I did this, however, I found that not much happened. It seemed to me (although I might be paranoid) that the same people came back but just under a different pseudonym and this time more abusive. I found it all very upsetting, but I was determined not to give up.

Before the park incident and my going online to give my opinions, Kevin and I discussed everything. But I knew that I could not discuss this with him. Also, I could not discuss my joining the Union and going to the meeting.

The meeting was online, and I was able to attend over Zoom from the office I shared at the State University. Looking at the participants it seemed that there were over 100 people online. The meeting very soon got heated with people saying that the pay we received was very poor and had not kept pace with inflation. Also, adjunct faculty had no rights, and the University were able to cut hours as they wished. We also did not have clear cut opportunities for promotion. Some members had been working for three or more years at the same pay scale rate. Additionally, not all members had health care coverage – this was dependant on a number of things including number of hours taught.

A person called Stan said he had been there for a few years and that he still had no rights. His hours had been cut for the spring term with no negotiation.

I spoke up from the written notes that I had made – arguing for more rights for adjunct faculty. I argued that we should have fractional contracts which would include holiday pay and sickness benefits. This led to an agitated discussion and Karl the Union rep promising to investigate further. Karl finished the meeting saying he was going to put a list together of our demands and take it to management. A strike was discussed if we did not have our demands met.

Another meeting was called for the same time next week.

I decided not to mention the meeting to Kevin in the car going home. However, I had had an email from Jenni saying that she was going for lunch at the "Olive Tree" restaurant with two friends on Saturday followed by an appointment at the nail salon. Why didn't I join them? I mentioned this to Kevin, and he seemed to think it was a good idea.

Kevin started talking about the research he was carrying out with John Strickland. He wanted to do some interviews of the public in the city and was looking for a researcher to carry this out for him. He was thinking of advertising online through the university intranet.

On Saturday I caught the metro to downtown and walked over to the Olive Tree restaurant. I was wearing a tunic top with black trousers. I thought I looked okay. However, when I arrived at the restaurant Jenni and her friends were already sitting at a table and called me over. Jenni looked glamorous as usual, and her friends were slim and beautiful. I thought older women were supposed to be fat and frumpy. This certainly was not the case with these three. Jenni introduced her friends as Keri and Jo. Jo had just got back from visiting a friend in Florida and had been working on her tan. Keri had been to a wellness spa in Arizona and talked about the benefits of a week of fasting and yoga. All three ate salads and drank sparkling water. I had wanted to order a burger when I read the menu but ordered a chicken Caesar salad as a compromise. I had wandered into a few clothes shops recently and decided I could not afford the prices (or fit into many of the clothes). However, it seemed to me that Keri was wearing an outfit I had seen in the Ann Taylor shop and Jo one from Tory Burch. They just looked so put together and vibrant. They had teamed their clothes with beautiful jewellery and subtle makeup. I just felt overweight and dowdy. They were perfectly nice and friendly, but I couldn't wait for lunch to end.

This feeling continued throughout my nail appointment. I was embarrassed where people were discussing the Spotify podcast where Meghan revealed that she had studied for the UK citizenship test. Apparently, she had asked her husband, the Prince, if he knew answers to some of the questions and he had said he had no idea! She really is making our Royal Family into a figure of fun, isn't she? People were laughing at him saying how dumb he is. I wished a hole would open in the salon and I could fall into it!! I willed my appointment to end soon.

I was so pleased when Janine suggested a coffee afterwards. She had invited Amara to join us as she was leaving at the same time. I rang Kevin to come and pick me up, as he had been to a football game south of the downtown area.

When Kevin arrived at the coffee shop and joined our table, I was ready to go home. However, he wanted to drink coffee and chat. He chatted to Amara and found out that she had dropped out of school. He asked if she would consider going back and then they got talking about his research and he asked if she would be interested in helping him as a research assistant?

I let the conversation go over my head. Since moving to this city, a number of things had started to bother me. Not least the way I looked. I knew that I had gained a few pounds through eating too much fast food, but I had always been a big-boned girl.

This had never concerned me previously. Kevin was a big person too and this had been what had attracted me to him initially. He felt safe and cuddly. I always felt that he would never judge me for my weight as he was big himself. However, today looking at him across the table I could see that he had lost some weight and had started to build up muscle definition from his evenings spent at the gym. I had dropped the gym quickly.

I told myself to stop worrying about my appearance – I had bigger concerns to address at present. The thought of being actively involved in a Strike appealed to me if that would address the issue of my having no rights and the University being able to cut my hours without negotiation. It may be that the Union could force the University to give us fractional contracts and then I would not have to worry about paying the bills in the new term.

This is what my head was full of as Kevin and I left the coffee shop and said goodbye to Janine and Amara.

Janine - alarm bells ring…

After my appearance on the Jerry Levens radio show I arranged to meet the new principal of the Institute for the Blind and Visually Impaired, Linda Lutz. She met with me and brought along her deputy, Arnold Spires. Linda was a large, vibrant person who liked the ideas for the mural and said I should go ahead with it. However, she said, the blind and visually impaired students who will attend classes here will not be able to see your mural and that is such a shame isn't it? I thought about this and agreed with her. She mentioned about tactile art for the blind. This is art that they can touch and feel and how certain museums are now running tours and making models of masterpieces that can be touched and felt by the blind. It was then that I remembered. Of course they were. I remember walking around the Tate Modern when I lived in London and seeing "Whaam!" by Roy Lichenstein and next to it was a much smaller version that was a raised image. I had asked the docent what it was and he told me that it was for blind and visually impaired visitors to touch and feel when they came on visits. It has been created by a British artist Heather Bowring. I realised then that I wanted the students of the Institute to enjoy my mural and I needed to give thought to how I could make my art more accessible to the blind.. I went away from the meeting feeling energised.

When I got back to the Cooperative I went online and tried to find out more about how to create tactile art. I could do a sculpture of the two musicians in clay or I could do a smaller version of the mural from other materials that blind people could touch. I read that this could be in tile, textiles, wood, metal, paper or plaster.

As the side wall of the Institute was on the road there was only a small sidewalk. I decided a sculpture to be placed next to the mural would not work. I therefore figured out how to make a small version of my mural out of plaster that I could mount on the wall low down for blind people to touch.

I was correct with my predictions about Amy and the running. She had found last week very difficult and was having problems keeping motivated. I had the number of our coach, Kathy, on my iPhone so I sent her a message asking what was the best thing to do? She recommended bringing Amy and Granny early to the session on Tuesday evening this week and she said she would get the Head Running Coach, Peter, to meet with them in a coffee shop across the street. I told Amy and Granny I would drive, and I went to pick them both up early and took them to the coffee shop. They seemed surprised when Peter joined us for a coffee. He asked how they felt about the running?

Amy responded that she ached all over and had found last week (where we had ramped up to three minutes running) very difficult. She said, previously she had not been doing much exercise and only recently had started to do the Robert John videos and workouts. However, in her opinion Robert John was relatively gentle with the workouts.

Peter sympathised and said he felt it was great that they were taking part. He asked granny how she had found it?

Granny said basically the same – upping the time to 3 minutes had proved very difficult.

Peter said that he understood that if someone had previously not been doing much exercise the program might be challenging. He said – can you walk the course? That is, can you walk briskly for 25 minutes without getting winded and breathless?

They looked at one another and it was obvious they did not know if they could do this. They had been breathless and winded after attempting to run part of the course, but could they walk it?

Peter then said he recommended that instead of running this week – we walk briskly for 25 minutes and find out how this affected us. If we ended up out of breath and exhausted, then we needed to keep walking until we had built that level of fitness up.

It was good advice but I wished someone had told us this before we started!! I felt that the Running Club should have helped us a bit more in this regard.

So this week we walked for 25 minutes with our coach, Kathy who encouraged us to walk briskly. The first evening was difficult, the second evening better and by Saturday morning we felt much more confident. So next week, we are going back to the "couch to 5k" training program.

On Saturday afternoon I went to the nail salon – I felt I deserved some "me" time. Ellie was there and it was very busy as usual. There was some discussion of the Spotify podcast by the Duchess of Sussex but most of the conversation was about the Mayor's plans for the city. I was quite excited about the idea of street art and joined in the discussions.

My appointment ended just as the salon was closing and I asked Ellie if she would like to join me for a coffee. Amara was also leaving, and she joined us.

We talked for a few minutes about my planned mural and then Ellie's husband, Kevin, joined us. He had been to the football and had stopped off to pick Ellie up to take her home. I had not met him previously. I knew he is a professor at the State University. However, he was more handsome that I had expected and in relatively good shape. I know Ellie had told me he had been working out in the gym.

When he sat down, he sat next to Amara, and I could not help but notice there seemed to be an instant attraction between them. He was much older than her, but I got the impression she liked older men. Ellie was holding forth about the changes in the city and did not seem to notice this.

Kevin asked Amara if she was attending school. Amara explained she had dropped out and Kevin asked if she had plans to go back. They got into a deep conversation about choice of majors and then onto to Kevin's upcoming research. Kevin told Amara that he needed an assistant to do some interviewing in the city centre for his research and he was going to advertise online unless Amara would be interested? Amara seemed very interested and they exchanged numbers.

Ellie seemed oblivious to this going on right in front of her. Perhaps I have a suspicious mind, but I would not want Gene doing research with a beautiful 21 year old Thai who looked at him adoringly!

I really hope I have this all wrong. I told Gene what I thought when we were in bed later. He told me to keep out of it. If Ellie did not seem concerned – what business is it of ours? He asked….

Amara – a way forward…

This was the week I learned cooking is fun and can be easy and I met a man who became very important in my life.

Mom was still inconsolable and was either in her room or sitting at the island in the kitchen drinking. I had given her some of my wages from the salon and that had helped pay the household bills she said. I found it hard to believe, that she could have spent all of grandad's money on a big house and now there was no money left, and as a result she now had to worry about affording to live in it. She also rambled on about when dad had left us before. This was some years ago when I was very young, and grandad was ill in hospital. Mom was visiting grandad, apparently, every evening and upset that his illness had turned terminal. One day she came home, and dad had disappeared.

"I'll never forget the day he came back" she said, "Grandad had only just died, and I was heartbroken and then there Somchai was ready to wrap his arms around me and make me feel loved again".

I could never understand why any woman would welcome a man back who had behaved so badly. I just let her ramble on as I started to cook in the kitchen. I had got the recipe for Thai Chilli Basil chicken from the internet and found it was easy to make.

As we sat eating it mom had to admit it tasted nice – although she had a number of critiques about the seasoning and the way I had "plonked" it onto the plate. "You have absolutely no finesses" she said "it doesn't look nice at all. You should set it out nicely…" blah, blah, blah. I stopped listening and left her to load the dishwasher.

On Wednesday as I came out of the salon dad came out from the shadows of the doorway of the Tory Burch shop next door and stood before me. He wanted to chat and to explain why he had left us. I went with him to a bar on the corner of The Walks and let him explain. He seemed more sober than usual. He had fallen in love with a wonderful woman and sadly he had to be honest and confess that love seemed to have flown away from his marriage to mom years ago.

I asked him where he was living, and he told me he had rented a loft apartment in the trendy River section of downtown. The woman he was in love with was a successful businesswoman, and they had a nice life together. I said that Jinni had told us that Randi was a hostess at the Black Cat bar and was this the same woman? He said that she wasn't just the hostess, she was a part owner in the bar and very rich. He said they had more money than they knew what to do with. He then gave me money and told me to go out and treat myself.

"Could I afford money like that if I was lying?" he said. "Randi is an heiress and businesswoman and the Black Cat is just one of her investments"

I really didn't know what to believe. It is hard to believe your father is a liar, but dad had been found out playing the "big man" so many times in the past. I decided not to challenge his fragile ego.

In the salon I had to appear smiling and interested in the conversations. There was still some talk about the Duchess of Sussex and her podcasts. She had talked about good wife/bad wife, and this was debated a bit in the salon. I can tell you that I don't intend to be a wife. If what my parents had is an example of a marriage, forget it. I'm also never having children.

On Friday, after I got the money from dad, I texted Vinny and we arranged to go out for a meal that evening to a Mexican restaurant in the downtown. Vinny was very chatty about the work he had been doing working virtually from home. This was work in the gig economy. He was helping a cool guy who owned a fitness company with his podcasts and client communication. This seemed to involve making captions for podcasts and looking for new clients on the internet via Instagram, Facebook, Twitter and TikTok. The pay was good he said but it was based on results rather than hours worked. Vinny mentioned that there was a website that had adverts for this type of work, and this is where he had found this opportunity. He was going to see how this work went before deciding whether to take on any more assignments.

I asked what benefits came with this work – and Vinny said there were none as it was the gig economy. He argued it was flexible working hours and as he lived at home his father had him on his health insurance. Vinny was very protective of his mental health well-being and did not want to work full time as this might be too much at the moment. His parents were supportive of his decision, as he needed time to find himself before committing to full time employment.

Vinny was still waiting for his first pay check so I paid for the meal and cocktails with dad's money. We drove back to my house, and I sneaked Vinny into my room. Mom was in her room with the TV turned up loud so had no idea Vinny was with us.

Saturday I was back to the salon working on nails and smiling and being friendly all day. As I was leaving Janine asked me if I wanted to join her and Ellie for a coffee. I went to the coffee shop with them. We had only been in there for a few minutes when Ellie's husband arrived. I knew he was a professor at the University, but I had not met him before. I immediately loved his floppy hair and smile. He is a big man but looked like he had been working out at the gym recently. When he looked at me, I felt butterflies in my stomach. This is stupid, I told myself. This man is old enough to be your father and married to a customer! When he talked to me and our eyes met, I felt shy and was worried I was blushing. I explained I had dropped out of UCLA. He wondered why? We discussed what I would study if I returned to university. Then he told me about the research he was carrying out and the fact he needed an assistant to help him do some of the interviews. If I was going to apply to go back to university and I could say that I had been a researcher during this time it would really be looked on favourably. He encouraged me to apply to be a researcher on his project. I said I would ask Jinni if I could have the time off from the nail salon to conduct the interviews. We exchanged numbers.

When I left the coffee shop, I felt happier than I had felt in months. I wanted to work with Kevin, and I wondered if he would pick my application if I was to apply…

Thai basil chicken

Ingredients:
2 or 3 tbs peanut oil

250g minced chicken

1 or 2 chopped small red chillies – remove the seeds if you want a less hot dish

2 or 3 cloves of garlic, peeled and sliced

½ a red onion, cut into small dice

1 tbs Sugar

2 tbs Soy sauce

2 tbs Fish sauce

A handful of basil leaves

Method

Heat the oil in a wok or wide frying pan at a high setting

Add the onion, garlic and chilli and stir fry for a minute or two

Add the chicken and cook, chopping up lumps to make sure it cooks evenly. You will need to move quite fast, as the high heat will burn the ingredients if you let it sit for long.

When the chicken is browned throughout, add the sugar, soy and fish sauce. Stir as the mixture comes to a boil, then add the basil leaves and stir until they have wilted.

Serve immediately with cooked white or brown rice

Chapter 8

November brings new opportunities….

After the Mayor had announced his strategy, work was started to put it into operation. This started with traffic being diverted south of downtown and onto the I-87 instead of going through Gent Town as it had done previously. It would be a long time until the area was converted into a beautiful boulevard, but this was the start and people felt optimistic.

The Mayor also spoke out that the work he was planning would bring jobs and work to the City. At present the official employment figures showing unemployment at an all time low and the Mayor said his goal was "zero unemployment".

The Mayor also announced his support of a local charity "Go higher" which provided scholarships to disadvantaged students so that they could attend University. He would be spearheading the raising of funds at a Charity Ball on December 17. This was to be a spectacular event in the downtown Hilton hotel sponsored by local businesses. Sponsorship had already been secured from the State University and also the international firm of accountants, Alex Gold.

At the same time, it was rumoured that an online retailer was planning to build a massive warehouse in the northern suburbs, which would also bring jobs to the city.

It seemed that the city was on an upward spiral, yet there were some worrying trends.

House prices and rents continued to rise and there were many people employed in the gig economy. The gig economy meant that people were employed on short term contracts without job security or, in most cases, benefits. There were rumblings of a possible strike at the State University about the payment of lecturers on short term contracts which meant that they had no rights.

In November 2022 reports began to appear in the Press that the Duke and Duchess of Sussex were about to release a documentary on the streaming service Netflix that contained revelations about the Duke's family in the UK. These revelations could prove to be even more scandalous than had been revealed previously. Rumours of racism and damage to mental health were put around. At the same time, the Duchess of Sussex continued to release weekly podcasts. These were discussed in the salon alongside events in the city. The Duchess had talked about activism for women – and how women get "no credit and all the blame". She said she was a campaigner for "women and girls" and that she reached out to women who are having a hard time in the media.

The Purple Orchid salon continued to be a hub of gossip and all of these subjects were discussed.....

Jinni - interferes and is threatened...

I spoke to my financial adviser about the possibility of leasing a store in the redevelopment area. She advised contacting the Mayor's office for more information on the redevelopment scheme, which I did.

The person I spoke to in the Mayor's office was very helpful and gave me information on who to contact regarding possible upcoming leases of business premises. She also mentioned about the Mayor's upcoming Charity Ball and asked if I was planning to support this event. I asked if she could send me more information.

I began to see a long-term strategy with my business expanding into the redevelopment area, with the possibility of adding a spa to our services. It was an exciting time for me.

When I received the email from the Mayor's office I looked through the information about the Charity Ball. I nearly passed out when I saw how much it was per ticket, but I realised it was for a good cause. I decided to buy four tickets for the event.

This was very expensive, but I felt it would elevate my position within the City. I would decide later who to invite.

That week Amara asked if she could speak to me in private. She told me about the opportunity to work on a research project for a professor at the State University. This would involve her spending one day a week for the next few weeks interviewing people and then writing up the results. She asked if she could apply and cut her hours back in the salon. I told her to go ahead. I agreed it was a good opportunity for her. I hoped if she was given the project that she did not blow it in the same way she had her university place at UCLA.

I knew if Amara cut her hours back, I would need someone to take her place. I had grown reliant on Amara over the weeks she had worked in the salon. She was a good, thorough worker who liked chatting to the customers. I immediately thought about Song, the new manicurist, who currently worked part time.

Later that week Amara told me that she had been successful in applying for the project at the University. She started next week. We agreed that Tuesday would be a good day for her to work on the project.

I had planned to speak to Song about working the extra hours, but I got a call from my accountants that afternoon. They do the payroll and financial accounts for the salon. I went into the back room to take the call.

"HI Jinni, this is Valerie Broxton. How are you?"

"I hope all is in order" I said "I know I was a little late sending over some of the documents this month"

"That is okay – but there is a problem with the payroll. It concerns your new manicurist Song. She still has not sent me her social security number as we requested. This made me a bit concerned. I decided to check the address you gave me. It appears to be the address of a vacant warehouse in Gent Town".

I felt sick – I am not stupid, dear. I know all about immigrants to the USA who are here illegally and do not have official paperwork and I do not employ them in my salon. I always insist that manicurists have their certifications and a social security number. I had seen the manicurist certificate, but Song had told me she had her social security number at home and would email that to my accountants. As we had been busy in the salon, I had completely forgotten to check if she had done this! I was really annoyed with myself.

Valerie went on "I cannot pay her without her social security number so please get her to send it as soon as possible. You may also want to check out the address she gave you. However, all of this has made me very suspicious, and I wonder if we should be paying her? It certainly seems to suggest that she may be here illegally.".

I thanked her for the information. I told her to process the payroll, but not to include Song.

When Song had finished her customer's nails, I asked to see her in the back room. I told her what the accountants had said.

"You shouldn't be working here in the US, should you?" I said

Song immediately broke down in tears, sobbing loudly. "Please don't let me go" she pleaded "I will starve without money from this job."

I thought that seemed a bit far-fetched and I asked where she was from and if she was in the USA legally?

I knew she was Chinese. She said she had come to the USA to attend College and had obtained a visa on that basis. This visa was a temporary visa. It did not give her the right to stay in the USA for ever. The purpose of the visa was to allow her to study in the USA and had very strict conditions attached to any paid work that could be obtained during the duration of the visa. She arrived in Los Angeles which was expensive. Friends told her to get a job that paid cash, and this would help her to pay her expenses. She had been working for a cleaning service as well as going to school. At college she had met another Chinese student, Lily, who was doing the same thing. Lily became her best friend. Both dropped out of college due to pressures of studying in a foreign language and working. Their visas would be invalid because they dropped out of college, so were now in the US illegally. They moved to this City to settle and work. Lily had found out on the internet that there were people in this city who could help them get forged papers so they could work in the USA. This was expensive and they had not been able to afford to get the documents yet. However, it was easy to forge a manicurist certificate and get a job in the salon.

"Please don't let me go, Jinni" she pleaded "there have been no customer complaints about me, in fact, I have received very good tips and people like me."

I found it hard to have empathy with her.

"What do your family in China think about you dropping out of college when they had most certainly saved and sacrificed so you could go to the USA? Do they even know?" I asked.

She told me that her father was the Dean of a college in Guangzhou. He was very intelligent and academic. He wished her to be an academic like him or a professional person such as an accountant or lawyer. She had found school very difficult and did not achieve the grades her father expected. It was only with calling in favours and paying an agent in China that he had been able to get her a place at a university in Los Angeles. Her father was not a rich man, and this had cost him a lot of money. Her poor academic performance continued at the college in LA. She felt that she had lost face before her family in China and was a failure in life.

I began to feel sorry for her at this point. I was never academic either and I know that parents can put a lot of pressure on their children to succeed academically.

I told her that if I continued to employ her I was in a lot of trouble with the Immigration authorities. I said I would think about what to do about the situation. I encouraged her to contact her family and to confess to what had happened. While I had a chance to think about what to do, she could stay, but I would pay her in cash. I gave her cash for the work she had done to date. I told her when she returned on Monday, I would have made my mind up about what to do about the situation.

That evening, I returned to my apartment and immediately rang Somchai to tell him about the situation. He put me on speaker phone so Randi could join in the conversation. Randi said that there were a couple of "wetbacks" who washed dishes at the Black Cat bar who did not have papers. They were paid in cash. Recently, a Chinese man had joined them, and it seemed he did not have papers either. The owner of the bar, Marlon, felt that it saved him money employing them as he did not have to fill out any of the paperwork or worry about the payroll.

I was shocked. I had always tried to follow rules and do everything legally. I knew also that Marlon liked these guys because they were cheap! If he paid cash, they had no rights and no benefits.

I asked if he worried about the Immigration Authorities? Randi said there had never been any trouble in the five years she had worked there.

I was in an absolute quandary about what to do. I knew I should let Song go and report her to the authorities, but another side of me worried about her. I knew what it was to have ambitious parents and to feel you could not live up to their expectations. Could I abandon her in a foreign country and not have this on my conscience? I decided to have a little glass of SangSom while I thought it over and eventually I fell asleep fully dressed on the sofa…

Ellie - Fighting for her own rights and the rights of others .

At work I continued to teach my classes knowing that I had only a few more weeks before my hours were cut drastically. I knew the Union were working on my behalf. They drew up a list of demands which they intended to show to the management. These were circulated to members, and we had another meeting. I spoke again talking up the benefits of fractional contracts that gave members health benefits and some protection against having their hours cut.

Karl, the Union Rep, then promised to put these demands to management.

I felt that it might be a good idea to publicize a possible upcoming strike and the obvious place was on the early morning commuter show. I rang Libby, Jerry Leven's PA and told her about the Union meeting with management. She promised to talk to Jerry about it. Apparently, Jerry thought this was a good topic for his show and invited me back to speak about it. Libby asked if I could talk on the phone with Jerry on Friday of this week. This was my day where I did not teach so I agreed to this.

I also wanted to speak out more about the various issues I had in my head and wondered if I could have a podcast of my own? I started searching around on the internet and found it was quite easy to record yourself talking and put up a video onto YouTube. Some people who had done this had many followers. I had to find a name for my broadcast and then I could post it. I called myself "An opinionated Limey". I first recorded myself talking about fat shaming. I started by reading out some of the comments that people had made about me after my picture appeared in the "local paper". These were cruel remarks about how in their eyes, I was fat and therefore should not give my opinion on local affairs. I then went on to talk about Susie Orbach who wrote "*Fat is a Feminist Issue*" over 40 years ago. In 2018 she spoke to a British newspaper (*the Guardian*) about her book which was a forerunner in talking about inequality. This inequality related to how obsessed some women got about the way they looked and their relationship with food. Women had been conditioned to believe that their value to others related to how sexually attractive they were and therefore stopped eating when they feared that they looked fat.

Some women have challenged the view on what it is to be beautiful – Susie says these women "stopped worrying and dared to live from our bodies". However, these women were up against the beauty industry which played on the insecurities of women. This included all the companies that introduced dieting and beauty treatments. In more recent years, there are cosmetic surgery apps and filters to apply to pictures on social media. Influencers with false breasts, lip and facial surgery and impossibly thin bodies. All designed to make the average woman feel inadequate and unattractive.

Susie says "If we weren't continually assaulted by the merchants of body hatred, we would not be so vulnerable to the assaults"

I argued, we are all different, we should all we accepted for what we are. I finished by talking about the National Association to Advance Fat Acceptance (NAAFA). This association holds an annual conference and helps people with healthcare, employment and education. The Fat Underground is an offshoot group in Los Angeles. They state the following:

> "We believe that fat people are fully entitled to human respect and recognition. We are angry at the mistreatment by commercial and sexist interests. These have exploited our bodies as objects of ridicule, thereby creating an immensely profitable market selling the false promise of avoidance of, or relief from, that ridicule. We see our struggle as allied with the struggle of other oppressed groups, against classism, racism, sexism, ageism, capitalism, imperialism, and the like" *("Fat Liberation Manifesto", Judy Freespirit and Aldebaran)*

I ended the video on this note and uploaded it to YouTube late on Thursday evening.

Kevin had already gone to bed and I went into the study and made the recording without him hearing. I was happy with the recording, I felt it stated my position and that of millions of other people as well. I went to bed and slept well.

The following morning, I appeared on the Jerry Levens show again. This time I talked about the conditions at the State University where staff worked on short term contracts and could have their hours cut at short notice. These were highly educated people, I argued, who had studied for years for their qualifications, yet they had little if no rights in the workplace. I cited some figures I had found in the "*Hechinger Report*". About 40% of faculty are part time. The report said that half earn less than $3,500 per course, or about $28,000 per year for a typical teaching load and this is equivalent to the federal poverty level for a family of four. Four out of five say they have difficulty covering their expenses and less than one half have benefits such as health insurance.

There was immediately a huge response to this with people phoning in. My views had caused division again. Some people agreed that it was not right to treat any worker this way. Others argued that University fees were high enough as it was, and the University should find ways to cut its staff bill rather than increase it by giving rights to temporary professors. Someone said if I was fed up with teaching why didn't I get a real job? I might have to do something there to earn my pay.

Someone called Steve called in and said that degrees nowadays were a huge con. Many were not worth the paper they were written on. It was about time university lecturers started teaching the students something worthwhile instead of moaning and whining. He continued by saying he was fed up with lefty woke types like the limey who spoke on the show.

I can assure you; it was a very lively discussion.

After the show I clicked onto YouTube and saw the comments about my fat video. There were already over a thousand clicks on the video and the comments were in the main very negative.

One person stated that his name was Jon and he was a medical doctor. In the USA he said 42% of the population are obese. This is not a feminist issue – it is a health issue. With weight comes health problems such as diabetes, heart issues and mobility problems to name a few. He said if I had seen what he had seen I would not have posted this video.

Another stated that it didn't matter what I said. Fat people were in the main very unattractive and he would rather spend the rest of his life on his own with just his dog for company than date a fat woman!

There were some comments in support. One person said they wished there were more modifications made to everyday things to help fat people who they felt were discriminated against. They suggested longer seat belts on planes or allowing large people to take up two seats.

And so it went on.....

I felt like I had a voice, and I made my comments known. I was not prepared for when Kevin arrived home. He walked in with a face like thunder.

"What on earth do you think you are doing Ellie" he shouted "have you no idea? That radio show, where you spoke up, will do enormous damage to the University. Surely even you can see that. Our recruitment figures are already down and now that people think there may be a strike it will affect them further. Why oh why did you have to discuss it on a radio station? You never even asked me!!" he blustered.

It seemed his Head of Department was furious about the broadcast.

"Did it never occur to you that this might threaten your future at the University" Kevin went on.

"Before you spoke on this radio show there had been strong hints that I was to be included in a group of professors who were going to the Mayor's Charity Ball. Now it looks like my ticket might go to someone else less controversial".

He was furious. I couldn't believe he cared about the Mayor's Charity Ball.

He got his gym things and stormed out of the house.

I thought about his comments and my feeling was that I had no regrets. I am not a chattel who has to ask her husband's permission to speak, and someone needs to speak up for the lecturers with no rights and for fat women who are discriminated against. I felt I had done the right thing . . .

Janine - Granny and Amy start to get healthy....

Granny and Amy are back on track now with the "Couch to 5k" and this week repeated week three. I am so impressed by their resilience.

Both are now starting to get really serious about getting fit. Amy told me that when her partner passed away and she started living on her own the most difficult thing for her was what to make for meals. Previously she had always had someone to cook for. This might be her partner or her children when they lived with her. Living alone there was the temptation to miss regular meals and snack all day. She often did not have lunch, but instead would eat cookies and snack on toast slathered with butter and marmalade. In the evening she might eat more bread and soup rather than cooking a meal.

Granny said she was much the same. Often in the evening she "meant" to cook, but the act of cooking for one made her sad and lonely, so she would instead snack on chips and dip or a baked potato with beans.

None of this sounded very healthy and it was a big surprise to me to learn they lived like this. Together we went online and found some healthy recipes that they could cook and I suggested that they eat together on one or two nights per week – perhaps after running. I also invited them over to my house for a meal on Sunday, so they could eat with Gene and I.

After running on Thursday evening Amy asked us back to her apartment and she made a vegetable stir-fry, which I really enjoyed.

It was good to see them on track with the running and now also eating more healthily.

This week I started to design the mural for the Institute for the Blind and Visually Impaired and also to work on the tactile picture that would accompany the mural. I was lucky to have an intern at our Cooperative called Mindy who was able to help. It was certainly going to be a big job.

I had asked Gene if we could visit Atlanta for the Living Walls Festival and to see the street art there and this weekend we went on a short trip.

The Living Walls Festival is held each year and artists add murals to Atlanta's walls watched by thousands of fans. Apparently, they have already added over 100 murals to the walls of the city. I visited many murals. One that stood out for me was the mural for the Adult Swim Mural Project by Ariel Dannielle "A Mirror of Everyday Life". This mural showed a beautiful positive image of two young black females sharing friendship and laughter talking on the phone while in the safe space of their rooms. I noticed how the murals emphasized the culture of the city. They were such a joy to see as you drove around the city.

I came back inspired to make my own mural a joy to see for people visiting the new regeneration district of the city.

Amara - Begins to get back on track....

I was so excited when I found out that I had been chosen to be Kevin's research assistant. I couldn't wait to go over to the University and meet with him and discuss my role.

We met in his office. It was messy and cluttered and full of books. I looked at the titles on the shelves and saw that he had his own PhD on his shelf. University of Warwick. Where was that I wondered? Then I remembered his wife is English and they had lived in England for a long time.

We had a nice long chat. My job is to interview people using a questionnaire that Kevin had developed. I would do the interviews in the downtown area of the city over a three-week period and then write up the results and give to Kevin.

I was to start almost immediately, and I felt this was a great opportunity for my future career. I was grateful to Kevin for giving me the chance to work in academia and for something to put onto my resume.

Mom approved of me doing the research and I heard her on the phone to Auntie Suzanne telling her that it was a very prestigious opportunity for me. Why did mom have to talk about me behind my back in such a nice way and yet never say anything nice directly to my face? It was a complete mystery to me.

Mom was still mourning dad moving out and it was very difficult at home. On Thursday she seemed a bit more cheerful when she explained that Keesha was coming home for the weekend and was bringing her new man friend, Barry Grossman, with her. Mom was very excited to meet him. It turns out he is a comedian who has a regular slot on one of the late shows. Keesha was a guest on "Catch It", a popular game show on prime time TV at the same time as Barry. They hit it off apparently and he asked her out for a drink after filming the show.

Janice, Keesha's mom had suggested that we all go out for a meal on Saturday evening to a new Mexican restaurant. She even said I could bring Vinny. Mom was over the moon.

"Barry is so funny" she said "he has the audience in stitches. To be able to take current events and see the funny side is a gift in my opinion"

It was nice to see mom happy for a change, so I agreed to go with her to the restaurant to meet Keesha and Barry.

On Saturday Vinny drove mom and I to the restaurant. Mom had explained that we would be sitting in a VIP section if Keesha and Barry were with us. I rather doubted that but did not want to contradict her. When we arrived Keesha and Barry and her mom, Janice were sitting in the back of the restaurant in a nice booth with mirrors above it. It certainly wasn't a VIP section – if such a thing even existed!

I did recognise Barry from the few times I had tuned into the show he was a regular guest on. He was older than Keesha and balding. He always appeared lively and funny on TV and it would be interesting to see what he was like in "real life".

After introductions were made mom asked Keesha how things were going with the TV series. It seemed that all was well.

Mom told Barry that she enjoyed his appearances on the show and that he always made her laugh. He seemed a bit dismissive of her comments.

He didn't seem very funny as we chatted. He talked about himself a lot and how he was hoping to put together his one man show and take it on tour across America. He would do this while "resting" from the TV show. I thought he seemed a bit full of himself, but Keesha seemed happy and was hanging on to his every word.

Keesha's mom Janice asked how my mom was. Mom said she was not great and really missing dad. We chatted for a while and then Keesha said that she had nearly finished filming season one of the soap opera. On New Years Eve she was going to hold her first ever big party for friends at her apartment near to the Studios. She thought it might really cheer mom up if we came to the party. Janice would come along too. We could stay overnight and get to see the City where the program was filmed. Neither mom nor I had ever been there.

Mom was over the moon. "Will Bronson Parker be there?" mom said, referring to the man who plays the vet in the series. "He is my favourite" Keesha smiled and said she hoped so as she had invited all of the cast to come along. It was going to be a big party.

Janice then brought up the Mayor's Charity Ball. Keesha had been invited as a local celebrity and would be sitting at a special VIP table with a party from the Mayor's office.

Vinny said that his father was a lawyer in the Mayor's office. He was also going to the Charity Ball and had taken a table there for his family and friends. I hoped that I could be one of the friends and go the Charity Ball.

Later in the evening a young person who said she was fourteen years old came and asked for a selfie with Keesha. Other than that, we were not disturbed in our booth

In the car going back mom went on about how kind and thoughtful Keesha was to ask us to the party. And so it was that despite us having no money (to hear her talk) when we got home she later took out her credit card and booked us flights to go to Keesha's party. She also booked us a room at the Marriott which was walking distance from Keesha's apartment. "We will have to share as money is tight" she said. Looking at the cost it still seemed expensive, but all I could think was how nice it was to see her happy.

Chapter 9

Taking a stand and being seen....

The city was busy in the run up to Thanksgiving. Families planned to get together and the stores sold out of turkeys. "The Purple Orchid" advertised a special "manipedi" for ½ price in the week before Thanksgiving. This was billed as being for busy people who want to spend an hour being pampered.

The Mayor's office was pleased with the reaction to the Charity Ball. It seemed that it would be a sell out as demand had been high for tickets. Also, there had been several enquiries about leasing stores in the regeneration area once that had been developed – showing positive interest in the regeneration project.

In Royal news, in November *the Daily Telegraph*, a British newspaper announced that the Duke and Duchess of Sussex were to receive the Ripple of Hope award in New York City on December 6. This was to be awarded for "taking a stand against structural racism within the monarchy." The event, in New York City, was to be hosted by Kerry Kennedy (John F Kennedy's niece). Ms Kennedy is quoted as saying

"They went to the oldest institution in UK history and told them what they were doing wrong, that they couldn't have structural racism within the institution: that they could not maintain a misunderstanding about mental health."

She then went on to say

"I think they have been heroic in taking this step."

Meanwhile the Duchess made her final podcast for Spotify. This time it featured men rather than women. Apparently, this was the idea of the Duke, Harry, who felt that men should be included. In this episode Meghan discussed her book "*The Bench*" and how it was about the softer side of masculinity she argued.

To be able to show that side of your personality does not make you any less of a man for doing so.

The magazine *Vanity Fair* commented that she also reflected that what had come out of the series had been ironic. Although it was audio "and you can hear my thoughts without any visual, I feel seen"

Jinni - To help or not to help?

In the following two weeks I worked hard in the salon – I had special offers for Thanksgiving both on nail treatments and on sales of the wellbeing treatments. However, inside my head I was in a quandary. I was worried about Song and what to do about her. She was still working in the salon – illegally and for cash but I didn't have the heart to let her go. She was a beautiful young girl in a foreign country. Without papers and no means of support, someone could take advantage of her. I took her to one side and asked her where she lived – I told her I knew she didn't live at the address she had given when she applied for a job in the salon. She told me that she was living in Gent Town but with six other Chinese people. They all shared a room in a building near downtown. I guess this would be in the regeneration area. There was a shower, but the heating did not work so seldom was there hot water. They slept in bunk beds in shifts in the room. I could only imagine the conditions she currently lived under.

One evening at my own home, I googled Guangzhou and found it was in the South of China, northwest of Hong Kong and on the Pearl River. The population was about 15 million people, and the language is Cantonese. However, many people also speak Mandarin. Guangzhou is famous for Dim Sum which is a dumpling containing various fillings. There are 21 universities in Guangzhou.

I asked Song if she would join me at my apartment for a meal one evening after work. I wanted to know more about her. It never occurred to me that this was wrong.

I cooked us a Thai green curry and we sat down and ate together. I said I had read there were 21 universities in Guangzhou. I asked which one her father taught at. It turned out it was one of the less prestigious universities, but he was Dean of the Business School. He could speak English and had helped develop links with universities in England and the USA. Song's grades were on the verge of what was acceptable to get into her father's university but with the help of an agent (which is common in China) and the payment of some money she was given a place. Her father meanwhile was developing links with a university in Los Angeles and wanted her to finish her undergraduate degree in America. Song had been really struggling in China and was really scared about a move to America. However, he had his way and again with the help of an agent (whom he had to pay a large sum of money to) she secured a place at a college in California. She was frightened to go but she did not know what else to do so she moved to America.

I asked how she found life in Los Angeles. She said that Americans were very different and had much more freedom than she had experienced in her own country. She had got talking to some Americans in the student café and their way of life was so far removed from what she had been used to that she found it difficult to communicate. They were from rich families who could buy them anything they wanted. She felt poor and foreign at the side of them.

Also, she noted that American students would speak up in class when they knew the answer to a question but they would also speak up and admit it if they did not understand the material. Song could not understand how these students could do this. She was frightened of losing face and was quiet when she did not understand. She would leave the class with her head spinning and unable to process the material that had been discussed. Sometimes the lecturer would ask her for her opinion and she did not know what to say. She didn't feel she should have an opinion. She had been taught previously to learn the material in a book not have her own opinions on it. The idea of critical thinking felt alien to her. She felt very nervous and lost in classes with people from another culture who behaved so differently to her.

As a result, she talked only to other Chinese students, and these became her friends. Also, the money her father had given her was not sufficient to live on in an expensive city like Los Angeles.

"Did you tell your father this?" I said "Surely, he would have helped you had he known".

She said she was too proud to tell her father. Her friend, Lily who was from Shanghai, was also suffering because she had not enough money to live in Los Angeles. They found out on the Chinese grapevine that there was a Cleaning Company in Reseda that would employ Chinese workers.

"Lily and I went to see them, and they gave us work cleaning homes for rich Americans." They were told that they had to work during the day while the owners were at work. Often, they had to miss class as they were working as cleaners. They listened to recordings of the lectures and tutorials and asked friends who had attended to go over the classes with them. She had been struggling when she was attending class but now she felt completely lost. Soon her grades began to suffer. The pressure was too much for her and this led to her dropping out of college.

When she left, I sat reflecting on the evening and felt only sorrow for her. She was such a beautiful girl and had got herself into such a mess. Her father was this controlling man who would punish her severely for dropping out of college so she felt she could not tell him. Yet how did he feel not knowing where she was? Also, her mother, how must she feel? I now knew which university the father taught at and his name. I could get in touch and tell him where his daughter was. Surely this would be the sensible thing to do. He could then come to America and be reunited with her and take her back to the safety of the family home. I did not have children, but what if she was my daughter? How would I feel? All of this swirled around in my head.

A couple of days later Song told me that there had been a shooting on the street outside the room where she was staying. A young boy aged 14 had been killed. It had been traumatic for his family and his mother had been outside all evening until the police had cleared the scene. Song seemed visibly shaken and near to tears. She also said that Lily was so scared that she had packed her things and left without saying goodbye. She was trying desperately to find where Lily had gone but had been unable to contact her.

I couldn't bear to see her so upset. I also couldn't bear the thought that she might try to find Lily and leave without saying goodbye. I might never see her again. I told her I would help her to find a nicer place to stay in a safer part of town. I knew about a room which was currently vacant over my friend's garage in the Northern suburbs near to me. I rang my friend and asked how much she wanted for the room. The rent sounded reasonable, and I felt that with a little help from me Song could live there.

We went together to view the room and it had a tiny shower room and a hotplate and fridge so Song could cook. It was in a leafy suburb with a view over my friend's garden. We agreed that Song could rent the room with me paying part of the rent.

When Song smiled and seemed happy – I was happy. I felt I was doing good helping her with the room and letting her work in the salon.

Somchai was shocked at my behaviour. "Be careful Jinni" he said "you have no idea if this girl is telling you the truth and you are becoming very involved with her. You will be in so much trouble with the Immigration Authority if they find out"

I knew he was right, and I decided I would write to her father and tell him where she was. However, first I had to feel she was safe and settled in her room……..

Ellie - finds her voice and speaks out....

In the week leading up to Thanksgiving a lot happened at work. The Union called another meeting where they informed us that they had met with Management. Our demands had not been accepted. There was a stalemate between the Union and Management. However, the Union had also approached the American Union of University Professors to ask if they would be interested in supporting our demands. The members of this Union were professors on permanent contracts who did not have to worry about being terminated at short notice. This Union was concerned about the fact salaries did not seem to be keeping up with inflation and members were being asked to do more for the same money. What they were most worried about were threats to tenure. In an American university tenure is sought after as not only is it a permanent contract it also guarantees the professor a position at the university until they want to retire. In fact, once a member of staff has tenure their contract can only be terminated if there are extraordinary circumstances. I believe that this system was developed so that professors could have freedom to express their scholarly opinions without worrying about getting on the wrong side of administrators or other staff in their department.

The American Union of University Professors decided to support us. The two Unions then agreed to go back to management with joint demands for better working conditions. Again, the demands were met with stalemate. A strike was looking more and more likely.

I had spoken to Niall about my YouTube video, and we agreed to make a joint video about the low pay musicians received when their music was played on streaming services. This was planned for the week after Thanksgiving. I was also planning another video this time promoting large (fat) celebrities who are saying that it is good to weigh more and to be happy in your own skin.

Kevin was not happy about my involvement with the Union and with my speaking out on the radio and my YouTube videos. In other words, he was very angry at me. Our drives to and from the State University were often made in silence. This was so different to how we used to be. I used to love being with Kevin and we would be chatting and laughing the whole time.

However, I had no regrets that I had stood my corner. I felt that I finally had a voice and was taking active steps to stand up for my rights. It was a good place to be in.

At Thanksgiving Jenni had invited us to her house. Niall was there and the four of us were going to have a turkey dinner. She looked beautiful as usual, in a cobalt blue midi dress that brought out the colour in her eyes.

After we had eaten, I helped her move the dishes into the kitchen. She asked how I was?

I told her that I had never felt better.

She said that she knew I wanted to speak out and it was good I was helping Niall to publicise the poor pay musicians received from the streaming services. She said she had also watched my fat shaming video on YouTube. She then said she did not agree with the sentiments I had put forward.

"Being overweight can lead to a lot of problems" she said "My late husband started to gain weight in his 50's and this led to diabetes, high blood pressure and heart disease. I could see him gradually getting sicker before my eyes. But he was in denial that his illnesses had anything to do with his weight. He loved rich food and wine and beer. I found out from his work colleagues after he died, if I tried to put him on a diet and send him to work with a healthy lunch pack he would cheat and order burgers and fries during his lunch break. He loved anything calorie laden to be honest."

She went on with tears in her eyes "He should be with us today. If only he had tried to eat healthier and exercised."

This was followed by an awkward silence as we loaded the dish washer.

"I wish you would go to the gym with Kevin" Jenni said, "He is looking good from working out but he tells me that you haven't been going with him."

"I hate the gym, Jenni" I said "I don't feel my worth is tied up with the way my body looks. Yes, I might have some excess weight by society norms but I am happy in my own skin. Why should I go to the gym when it is so tiring and exhausting? I work hard and when I get home I just want to relax."

She was looking at me and I realised I was blabbering on – talking rubbish really.

To be honest I did feel aware of my stomach which was hardly washboard thin and my thighs which were rubbing against each other under my dress. When I dropped a fork on the floor, I felt embarrassed to pick it up in case she saw my massive bottom and this provoked another "pep talk".

That evening when we got home, I went into the bathroom to undress. I would not normally get onto the scales in the evening after a big meal, but I thought, what the hell, and went ahead. 220 pounds. Good heavens I thought. I didn't realise that the weight had crept up so quickly. On the plus size my breasts looked large, but when I looked again, these were sitting on quite a large tummy. It was my bottom that was the worst bit – massive would be the word to describe it. But then didn't Kim Kardashian have a big bum and men fancied her?

I had read that an estimated 70% of adults in the USA are considered either overweight or obese. It was becoming more normal in my opinion to weigh more. We should all be able to enjoy our food and not have to continually worry. However, was it attractive? I couldn't remember the last time a man had made a pass at me. I found Niall very attractive, but it had been all business with him. He hadn't even flirted with me. Of course, he had beautiful Jenni to go home to. Still beautiful in her 60s. I thought about men at work who always seemed to be friendly but only about work. Of course none of it mattered to a feminist I told myself. I should not see my worth in how men see me. I put my nightie on – it was hardly sexy but at least it covered up parts of me I didn't want Kevin to see.

I went into the bedroom – Kevin was either already asleep or pretending to be asleep. Gone were the days when he couldn't' wait for me to join him.

I was now a feminist and activist and that was where my worth lay. Perhaps I would try to cook more healthy food. I thought about what Jenni had said and I couldn't have Kevin getting sick like his father. However, it was a big no from me to the gym, I was pleased Kevin was going regularly to the gym though. However, for me I really didn't have time for that sort of stuff. I had so much more on mind that I wanted to share with the world.....

Janine - living her best life....

In the weeks leading up to Thanksgiving Gene had talked to me about his partnership prospects at Alex Gold, the international firm of accountants where he worked. Apparently, in the week of Thanksgiving after a partner meeting he was told that this had been green lighted. He was delighted with the news and accepted the offer of a partnership. A promotion announcement was to be made in January 2023 to everyone at Alex Gold.

I was thrilled for Gene, and I knew this would make a big difference to our future. We talked about changes we felt we should make because of this promotion. Our home in the Southern Hills area of the city was relatively modest. It was a two-bedroom two-bathroom townhouse in a gated community. We talked about moving up to a more substantial property. We had started to look at listings online. Kara who I knew from the nail salon had just started to work at Sun Hills Realty after obtaining her real estate license. She did not have any listings of her own but was able to help us with arranging viewings.

We discussed this in the nail salon when I went for my appointment. Everyone had ideas about properties that were for sale, and which was the best neighbourhood to buy in. We wanted to stay in the Southern Hills area but were flexible about which part. I had spent evenings and spare moments on "Zillow" and "Trulia" websites looking at homes. I felt we were so blessed to be able to move to a beautiful home and to live in such a lovely area.

We had planned the viewings of a few properties for the weekend after Thanksgiving. Meanwhile I continued to work on my mural for the wall of the Institute for the Blind and Visually Impaired, which was beginning to take shape. I planned to start work on the wall itself in December.

Granny and Amy and I continued with our "Couch to 5k" training. On Thanksgiving Granny had us all over for a meal. She said she felt she had so much more energy now that she was training and was able to cook for everyone without getting tired.

We ended up viewing two houses on the weekend. One was near to downtown in the historic district. It was a beautiful house with a stone façade that had been extended to include a wall of glass at the back. There were 3 bedrooms and 3 bathrooms. The greenbelt was behind the house, so it was not overlooked and there was also a decking area to sit out on. The owners had strung lights between the live oaks in the garden and it would make a lovely place to enjoy al fresco dinners or barbeques.

We then drove to the Southern Hills and to the Albion Country Club area. We drove up to the prestigious Copper Ridge Lane. We saw a beautiful large new home there with 5,000 square feet of living space. It had 5 bedrooms and 5 bathrooms and a media room. The main living area had vaulted ceilings and a fireplace for cool winter evenings. Gene whispered "this is a real family home. I can see it full of children laughing and playing. Just perfect for us in the future."

I could see that this would be a perfect family home, but I also felt sick thinking about this. Although Gene and I had been together for 7 years now, we had never had children. Since we returned to the USA from England, we had stopped using contraceptives but nothing had happened. What if we were infertile and could never have children? What if we bought a big home and then rattled around in it, just the two of us, because the baby we hoped for never happened? We were getting older too, and my biological timeclock was ticking away.

These thoughts put a cloud over what should have been a perfect sunny day...

Amara - beginning to see a way forward....

By Thanksgiving I had started work on the research project. I was enjoying interviewing people who, in the main, seemed happy to answer the questions and give me their views at the end. I had also devised a way to write up as I went along. I kept in contact with Dr Kevin, so he knew what was happening with my contribution to his research. He said he would come downtown next week, and we could go for a coffee after I had finished interviewing. I couldn't wait. I was genuinely happy helping him.

In other areas of my life, I was not as happy. In the salon, I overheard Janine discussing with Kara her intentions to move to a bigger house. She was so lucky to be able to afford a beautiful home and I thought about mom and her worries that we could no longer afford our home with dad gone. I hoped that things would turn out well in the future.

When I got home that evening mom was sitting in the kitchen with her laptop out on the kitchen island. She seemed miserable as usual. "It is a good job that your Uncle Alan and Auntie Betty asked us to go there for Thanksgiving" she said "I can't afford to buy a turkey, so it would have been very embarrassing if they were due to come here."

We alternated hosting Thanksgiving every other year

"I agree" I said, "especially as you can't cook and dad always did the cooking."

"There is no need to be like that" she said "If you only knew the mess he has left me in. I am having to use a credit card to pay for everyday expenses. How could he do this to me?"

I had bought some food, so I made a very easy pasta chicken dish and we ate that. After we had finished eating mom's phone rang and, guess what, it was dad.

I could only hear her side of the conversation, but she started off by being pleasant asking how he was and when was he coming back? When it seemed obvious, he was not coming back the conversation turned nastier and nastier. Eventually she hung up on him.

He had not told her his address, but Jinni had told her that Randi, his new lady friend, worked at the Black Cat bar. I had seen dad and he had told me this and dad often went into the bar while she was working so that was the place to catch up with dad.

The next evening mom asked me to go with her to the Black Cat bar. She insisted she had to see dad and convince him he had to give us some money. At first, I told her no, but I could see she was nervous and anxious and was going to go whatever I did. I felt if I went with her, I might be able to look after her.

Mom put the address of the bar into the satnav, and we set off. The bar was in a very dodgy part of town. It was wedged between a convenience store and a boarded-up shop. "Make sure you lock the car, mom" I said. I was not sure it would still be there when we came out.

The bar smelled none too clean and was decidedly rundown. A few men sat on bar stools and a blousy blonde was behind the bar. I assumed that was Randi. Dad was sitting nursing a whiskey at the far end of the bar. He did not see us immediately when we walked in. A fat old man who was near the door leered at me "Why hello" he said "and who are you? There is room for you next to me…" he indicated a vacant bar stool. I smiled and said "we are here to see someone thanks" Mom had seen dad and we made a beeline for him. When dad saw it was us, he looked sick. He exchanged a glance with the woman behind the bar. He got off the stool and said "Barb, Amara. What a surprise" Mom went straight up to him. "We need to talk now" she said.

Dad ushered us into a booth in the back of the bar. It was near the restrooms which were absolutely disgusting. Someone staggered out of there obviously high on something and when the door opened, I nearly gagged on the smell. What a dump. Who in their right mind would give up a beautiful home in the Southern Hills to sit in this place night after night? Dad indicated to the woman behind the bar and she brought us over two beers. Mom looked at her and said, "Aren't you going to introduce us Somchai?"

Dad shook his head and the woman left quickly.

"Is that her? The woman you left me for?" mom said. Her face was bright red, and she was near to tears. Now that we were in the bar confronting dad all her bravado seemed to have gone. I almost felt sorry for her.

"Barb, knock it off. I will give you money" dad whined "I told you that when we talked and you know I promised and I always keep my promises, but I have to get the money first"

I also almost felt sorry for him he seemed so pathetic. What a pair! Neither seemed able to do anything positive. In the end he got his wallet out and gave us 50 dollars in cash. He said that was all he had.

Randi meanwhile stood behind the bar and stared at us. If looks could kill.

I felt none too safe in this rundown place. The men at the bar didn't look like the types I would mix with and we were attracting attention the longer we stayed there.

Dad promised to give us 500 dollars on payday. I knew he didn't earn much and that would seem like a lot to him. I hoped he could still pay the rent wherever he was now. After this evening I was 100% sure it was not in a trendy loft in the Riverside area of the city. Mom accepted his offer as it was better than having nothing which was what she had at present.

I managed to drag mom out then without her having a go at Randi. Fortunately, the car was still there, and we drove home.

When we got home, I got undressed and ran a very hot shower and stood under it for a long time. I was now determined to go back to school to get my degree. I wanted to be independent and not reliant on any man.

At Thanksgiving we went to Uncle Alan and Auntie Betty's house and took a pumpkin pie as our contribution. Uncle Alan and Auntie Betty had cooked us a delicious turkey dinner. The downside was they wanted to have their say about dad. They made several remarks which were decidedly racist.

"This is what happens Barb when you marry a foreigner" Uncle Alan said "they don't have our morals or values. I heard all about Thailand on a program on late night TV. They have beach resorts where men dress up as women and have sex with tourists. They just want sex all the time and booze" he went on while drinking a whiskey "let's face it Barb Somchai used to come here and booze it up every year. When was he ever sober?"

Auntie Betty joined in, and I just wanted to run away. I felt defensive of dad – I know he is not the best dad in the world, but he is my dad and I don't like him being talked about in this way.

I made an excuse and went outside and sat on my own on the stoop. I wondered where dad was and what he was doing. I sent him a message to say, "Happy Thanksgiving" and he rang me. He was a bit worse for wear, but we had a little chat. He had cooked Thai food for Randi for Thanksgiving, and they were now watching TV in the apartment. He was a mess, but I loved him and I was glad I spoke to him on Thanksgiving.

I had made my mind up that this time next year I would be far away at a little liberal arts college in New England surrounded by intellectual types......

Pasta recipe

This recipe can be served with any kind of pasta, which should be cooked according to the directions on the package, but bow-tie pasta makes a nice base to absorb the creamy sauce..

Ingredients
2 tablespoons of olive oil (no need to use extra virgin).
1 medium onion, cut into very small dice
2 cloves of garlic, minced or crushed
200 grammes of sliced, skinless and boneless chicken thigh fillet
1 pack, about 250 grammes, of chestnut mushrooms, thickly sliced
10 grammes of dried porcini mushrooms, soaked in enough boiling water to cover. Leave for a half hour and then drain, reserving the liquid. Finely shop the mushroom.
150 ml Crème fraiche
Salt and black pepper to taste
10 grammes fresh basil leaves
Parmesan cheese for grating

Heat the oil in a wide pan and add the diced onion. Keep the heat medium, or lower if the onion begins to brown. You are looking for a uniform translucent mass, as the finished sauce should be pale in colour.

After about 5 minutes, when the onion is soft and cooked, add the sliced chicken and mushrooms and increase the heat a little as you stir fry the chicken and mushrooms with the onion mixture until the chicken has turned white and no pink is visible.

At this point, add the garlic and stir around until the garlic is cooked.

Add the crème fraiche and stir to combine, along with enough of the reserved liquid from the mushrooms to keep the mixture fluid. Simmer the mixture whilst the pasta cooks.

Adjust the flavour by adding a little salt.

Once the pasta is cooked, drain it and add it to the pan containing the chicken mixture, stirring to combine.

Serve topped with some grated parmesan and black pepper. Scatter some torn basil leaves over and serve.

Chapter 10

The Mayor's Charity Ball

In December preparations ramped up for the first ever Mayor's Charity Ball in the City. This was due to be held on December 17. By the beginning of December all seats sold out and it was expected to raise a substantial amount for the charity "Go Higher". The Mayor felt that events such as this coupled with his plans for the regeneration of the downtown area would help to publicise the City in the national press and give it new status and standing.

This view was not shared by all the residents. There were four murders in Gent Town during this same period that had not been solved. Muggings and robberies in the area continued also. Jerry Levens continued to discuss this on his commuter radio show prompting a lot of call-ins from residents with views to express.

It seemed now more and more likely that there would be a strike at the State University. The Unions and the management had so far failed to reach an agreement. This was also discussed on the radio and in the local news.

Little was said in public though in the city, about another growing problem which was the problem of illegal immigrants. These included people from south of the border, Mexico and S America. However, surprisingly, in recent months (since 2021) it had been reported in the *Daily Mail* that there had been Chinese nationals crossing the border. There were

"1,970 arrests recorded during the 2022 fiscal year, and just 323 the year before"

If these people were successful in their border crossings, they had no paperwork and worked at jobs where they had no rights or benefits and were paid in cash. As there was little publicity given to this issue in this city, the size of the problem was not immediately apparent. However, there were rumours that there was an underground site on the internet that was advising immigrants that did not have paperwork to reside and/or work in the USA to come to the city. In the city there were a number of employers willing to pay cash and ask no questions and the internet site could help with providing contacts.

After the Duchess finished her Spotify podcasts a huge publicity campaign was mounted by Netflix to publicise the upcoming documentary "Harry and Meghan". In this documentary the duo were reputed to drop more "bombshells" about the Royal Family. They were to tell their own story of their complex journey from senior Royals to their present life in California in their own words. Harry would also talk about growing up Royal and in the public eye. There were to be six episodes. Again, this proved to be very divisive. However, the comments people posted to the trailer put online by Netflix advertising the series were in the main negative. Below are a sample.

One commentator observed "I love the part where they say they hate the hierarchy in the monarchy and still keeping the titles Duke and Duchess.,"

Another observed "I love the part where they complain about being cut off financially at age 40....whilst the rest of the world struggles with food and heating....such amazing people....everyone's left eye wept for them."

Another commentator observed "I love the part where Netflix actually had the balls to leave the comments open. It's pure gold."

Jinni – a Charity Ball and falling in love...

I planned to go to the Mayor's Charity Ball on 17 December and I had invited three close friends to go with me. I went to the Tory Burch boutique next door to choose a dress. I wanted to look glamorous for the evening and feel like a member of society in the city. I was excited looking forward to the event.

The only thing was that I was still employing Song and paying her cash knowing full well that she did not have papers to work in the USA. Also, knowing that her parents were probably worried about her and not contacting them preyed on my mind.

On the Tuesday evening I was sitting in the back room for a few minutes rest before I left to catch the metro. I poured myself a glass of SangSom and sighed with relief that another day was finished. As far as I knew everyone had left and there was just me in the salon. I was shocked when the curtain opened and Song popped her head around.

"Hello dear" I said "I thought you had left."

She looked so beautiful – her hair was hanging loose and she had little or no make-up on. She walked over to my chair and began to massage my shoulders. At first, I tensed up, but I was tired, and she was an excellent masseuse.

"I know you are tired" she said "you work so hard. Let me rub your shoulders and help you relax."

"You can do that every night, dear" I teased. I wished she would. I knew as I locked up and we left for the evening, I would never turn her over to the authorities or tell her parents despite it preying on my mind. I just wanted her to be near to me. I would look after her, I told myself.

The following evening I had a different visitor – Somchai. Apparently, Barb and Amara had been to the Black Cat bar asking for money. He had promised to give them $500 when he got paid next time, but he was absolutely broke and down to his last few dollars. I let him talk. I had heard all this before from Somchai. He does not earn much and had rent to pay on the apartment he shared with Randi. It may very well be true that he couldn't afford to also give money to Barb and Amara. I wondered why he was so impulsive and never thought about the consequences. In the end I gave him the money, emphasising this was a loan and he had to pay it back with the other money I had already loaned him.

I was depressed when I got off the metro and I decided to do something completely out of character. I bought a bottle of wine and went around to Song's room. She was on her own when I arrived but didn't seem that surprised to see me. She was settling in fine, and the room was neat and tidy.

This time when she started to massage my shoulders it didn't stop at that. I spent the most wonderful evening and when I left to return to my own apartment in the early hours of the morning I felt more happy and more contented that I had felt in years.....

Ellie discovers family....

The week after Thanksgiving we received the insurance pay-out for the ring that was stolen. It was a relief to me to get the money as it meant we would not have to worry if I could not find extra work in January after my hours were cut. Kevin seemed relieved too and we had a surprising brief reconciliation. It was so surprising and swift that we forgot to use a condom. I didn't care though, it just felt nice to be desired again and we fell asleep in each other's arms.

The reconciliation did not last long when Kevin found out that I was going ahead with making another YouTube video with Niall this week.

"Can you not leave these things well alone, Ellie?" he asked. "The internet is an evil place where people can make comments that they would never dare make to a person's face. Why you would want to set yourself up for comment is beyond me. Why not do something more constructive if you have time to spare?"

I decided not to ask what he meant by more constructive, but I went ahead with the video anyway.

I felt Kevin and I were drifting apart. He went to the gym regularly now and I was beginning to see the difference this was making to his body. He was much more toned and fit. He was also busy with his research and spoke to Amara quite frequently about the role she had as his assistant.

It seemed at work that a strike was almost inevitable now. Management was at a stalemate with the Unions. This also annoyed Kevin as he felt that I was involved with the Union and a strike would be a disaster for the University. This was something else we bickered about.

Kevin was not chosen to go to the Mayor's Charity Ball either – he blamed this on me being involved with the Union.

So overall not a good time for our marriage.

However, at this time I also sensed an opportunity to get more attention for my videos. I saw that the Duke and Duchess of Sussex were about to release their documentary "Harry and Meghan" on Netflix and I could see from the advance publicity that this was going to be very controversial. The couple was going to tell their story in their own words about why they left the UK and ceased to be working Royals. It appeared to allege cruelty from his family. It was a tale about alleged racism and invasions of privacy and mental health issues played out against a backdrop of private jets, mansions and expensive clothes and jewellery. What more could you wish for to provoke controversy and discussion?

I knew that the Duke and Duchess were often discussed in the nail salon. I smiled when I remembered that Jinni did not know who they were, and this had prompted my first chats with Kara and Janine. Then I remembered that it is punishable with a fine or prison in Thailand to disrespect the royal family.

I had listened to some of the Spotify podcasts the Duchess of Sussex made. However, these did not speak to me in a way that made me want to comment or join in the discussion. In my opinion the Duchess did not so much interview her guests as talk about herself and her own feelings. I felt it was the relationship with the Royal Family that people were really interested in. I felt that a YouTube video on this topic would help elevate my status on YouTube. I might even get a following. There had been several comments to the videos I had already made but these were minor compared to the number of comments to any article or video about the Duke and Duchess and their relationship with his family in the UK. I intended to structure my video around the theme of the family.

Before I go any further with this plan, I should explain a little more about my own family in England. I grew up in Yorkshire.

My mother was a nurse who contracted cancer and died while I was studying for a master's degree. I had one brother who then emigrated to Australia. Dad had always been quiet and somewhat distant from myself and my brother. Within a couple of years, he had remarried to a woman named Joan. The marriage only served to put more distance between us. I put all my energies into my marriage to Kevin and did not see my father often. By the time Kevin's father died and we decided to move to the USA my visits home were limited to about two per year. Once in the summer and once at Christmas. Now that I was in the USA I very rarely heard from dad. We did FaceTime at Christmas and on birthdays. The same with my brother who now lived in Sydney, Australia with his Australian wife.

I was therefore very distant from my own family. I had had no qualms about moving to the USA and leaving dad and his new wife behind in England. I did not intend to mention any of this in the YouTube video. Rather I would concentrate on the duo's complaints about the Royal Family and how they were treated. I felt this would be sure to provoke comment.

So, in addition to the YouTube video with Niall about musicians, and one about fat celebrities I also made a third video about the "Harry and Meghan" Netflix documentary. I released all three quickly, before the documentary was released on Netflix. As expected, the British newspapers had already stirred up a lot of heated comments about the duo. In addition, Netflix had released a trailer which also stirred up comments.

When I told Kevin what I had done, he was now furious.

"Why would you want to release a video about those two?" He complained.

In Kevin's view they were just a "flash in the pan" and once they had spilled their secrets would be forgotten quickly as the public moved on to other topics. He also argued that as the USA did not have a monarchy many Americans had better things to think about than what was happening to the Royal Family in the UK. I argued that the duo was part of history as they had attacked a centuries old institution in my native country and as such were worthy of attention. I felt I was doing the right thing at the time as I got many more comments on my video on the duo than on the other two videos I had made. However, again this put me into the centre of something divisive and controversial, and again it made me feel alive and noticed. I craved the attention and would not listen to Kevin.....

Janine - a new home and running faster.....

We have now found our dream house. When we drove up to the house we knew even before we went inside that this was going to be our home. It was in the Southern Hills. The home was on Southern Springs Lane which is near to the golf course (for Gene) and to the Vinings Village shopping centre for me. There are also stables just down the road and horse and running trails. The house itself has hardwood floors and coffered ceilings on the main level. There is a beautiful great room with a wall of glass overlooking the rear terrace. The owner's suite has a fireside sitting area and a beautiful bathroom. But for me the best feature of the house is the top floor which has a bonus room filled with light which I know I can make into an art studio. It is a large home with 4 bedrooms and 4 bathrooms, and I hope that one day it will be filled with the shouts and laughter of children. I decided to think positively.

Kara, who I knew from the nail salon, had shown us the home, but it was not her listing. I believe that she would receive some commission from our purchase of the house. I was pleased to be able to help her in her new career as a Real Estate agent.

We put our townhouse up for sale and were thrilled when it sold for the full asking price within a couple of weeks.

It was an exciting time. I was working on the mural for the Institute for the Blind and Visually Impaired and hoped to begin painting the wall in December. In connection with this, the Mayor's office had asked if I could complete the wall by the 17

December for the Charity Ball. A picture of the mural would be on display at the Ball. Also the piece of tactile art would be shown at the ball, as an innovative way to help blind and visually impaired people appreciate art. I was also asked if I would take part in the silent auction. The rules for a silent auction are different to a regular auction and should put less pressure on people to take part. Items are donated to the auction and shown to people at the Charity Ball. There is a bidding app that can be accessed through your iPhone for people to submit their bids anonymously. A member of staff from Alex Gold who are sponsoring the event, would access the bids and decide who was successful. Then I was to announce who had been successful in bidding for the various items. I was really looking forward to the evening.

Also, I was still running with granny and Amy. We had walked the course briskly and repeated a week, so we were now up to week four. This week was a mixture of walking and running for 25 minutes but included two five minute running times. I wondered if they would be able to do this. Also, although I did not say this out loud, I also wondered if I would be able to run for five minutes. We met with our coach, Kathy, who always accompanied us. Kathy made sure that we stretched before the run began – she suggested about five minutes of warming up. She also recommended pilates or yoga to help develop strength and balance. She felt as we progressed with the running that these would help us strengthen our core.

I was beginning to see this as a package now – healthy eating, pilates, yoga and running. No matter what age you are that was the way forward to a better life.

We did make it through week 4 but again granny was worried we were “shuffle running”. Not really picking our feet up and shuffling from foot to foot. This meant that we were effectively running but not very fast!

We had so far to go yet before we would be able to try a 5K run.

Amara - an inspirational mentor....

I was still working on the research project and had arranged to meet Dr Kevin for a coffee to discuss progress so far. We sat together in a booth in the back of the coffee shop. I had some questions on the work I had done so far. Kevin listened and had good advice for me. I loved how knowledgeable and intelligent he was and the way he responded to my questions. He also told me to stop calling him Dr. "Call me Kevin" he said, "there is no need to be so formal".

I enjoyed the time we spent together and was thrilled when he suggested another meeting in a couple of weeks.

"Same time, same place" he said.

I couldn't wait. He was an attractive man and so clever. Who wouldn't want to spend time with him, I asked myself.

On Wednesday of that week, when I got home from the nail salon, I could hear voices. I went through to the kitchen/family room. Dad was sitting on a kitchen stool laughing and flirting with mom. Mom was laughing along with him. His jokes were terrible and so out of place under the circumstances.

"Here she is" said mom smiling at me.

"I hear you've been cooking" said dad "inspired by me, huh?"

"Why don't you cook tonight Amara" mom said, "and dad can stay and eat with us?"

I knew he had brought the $500 so that would be part of the reason she was in such a good mood. However, the thought of cooking for a man who had left us for another woman made me feel physically sick.

"Can't sorry" I said, "I have arranged to meet Vinny this evening".

I went up to my room and had a quick shower and left as soon as I could. Dad was still in the kitchen laughing and joking. How ridiculous.

I had texted Vinny while I was showering and changing, and he said to come over and we would go out for something to eat.

When I arrived at his home, his mother was sitting in the family room watching TV. Vinny introduced us. His mother was a severe looking woman and not friendly, in my opinion. She was a partner in a law firm downtown.

"So, what do you do, Amara?" she asked

I told her I had had mental problems and had dropped out of UCLA and was working in my aunt's nail salon until I felt better and was able to go back to pursuing a career.

The way she looked at me made me feel guilty and bad about myself. I realized I was gushing trying to explain myself.

"I was first in my family to go to university......It was difficult to manage financially in Los Angeles and I had to take a job....... juggling the job and my studies was too much and I had a mental breakdown......I am now feeling better..... I am working on a research project one day per week for a professor at the State University....I am planning to go back to School next academic year..."

"I wish you all the best" she said "Vinny is also going to go back to school".

It was the first I had heard of Vinny going back to school Also, Vinny was acting like a 10-year-old in front of his mother and "the cat seemed to have got his tongue" as the old saying goes. I then realised that it was most certainly his father that indulged him and allowed him to live at home and work in the gig economy while he found more permanent employment.

We escaped as soon as we could, and I drove down to "The Cattleman's" a steak house in Vinings Village, an upmarket shopping district in the Southern Hills.

I asked him how his online job was going. It didn't seem to be going well as he was paid on results, and it had been very difficult to sign people up to a health and fitness app. He then told me that his mom had signed him up for a one-year course to gain a Certificate in Paralegal Studies. This course was being taught in Washington DC and after it finished there was a job waiting for him in the Washington office of her law firm. The course was starting in January.

I asked if this is what he wanted to do. He said he wasn't 100% sure but he had grown fed up hanging about the house working in the gig economy, so it was something. He felt if he got the certificate, he could always quit the job if it got too much for him. He was concerned about the salary though – he had read that the average salary for paralegal professionals is $51,000. He felt this was very low and he could not imagine how he could live on such a low salary.

"Take my parents' house" he said "one sold down the road for $850,000 last week. How could I afford to live in a house like the house I grew up in on a $51,000 salary? But why should I have to settle for less than I am used to? I can't go to law school as I don't have the grades" and he stopped there and smiled "or the inclination. The thought of working like my mother and father do is not appealing either. I do not want to settle. I want the best, such as a good career, a big salary and a happy life. My degree is in Media and Communications. I found out too late that the Public Relations industry is highly competitive. I applied for jobs but didn't get any interviews when I was at university. Many of the jobs in Communication and Marketing are in the gig economy. It is possible to get a job, but I have found that it is very difficult to make any money at all. I feel our generation is screwed."

I felt there was more to this than he was telling me. I guessed his mother was tired of supporting him and wanted him to do something productive. He didn't seem very happy about it though and that was not a recipe for happiness.

I would miss him when he moved to Washington DC, also my mom worked at the local TV station. I wondered if she knew if they needed people to work in communications or Public Relations (PR). If Vinny could get a job here, he would not need to move to Washington DC. I decided I would ask her when I got home. It was an area I had never been interested in personally.

When I got home dad had gone. I mentioned to mom that Vinny was interested in a job in PR. She did not seem very positive. She said Vinny was correct, decent jobs in PR and advertising were very hard to come by. However, it was possible to get jobs through the gig economy to get your foot in the door. She said celebrities used agencies to do their PR for them and perhaps Vinny should try applying to one of the agencies. She mentioned the PR agency, Sunshine Sachs and said, "look what they did for Meghan Markle and Prince Harry". She went on to say how the couple had got multi-million-pound deals at Netflix and Spotify.

I messaged Vinny about this, and he agreed working for a PR agency like Sunshine Sachs would be a great career but he knew that the competition was intense. I wondered if Keesha knew anyone and could help him get an "in" at a PR agency or a film studio. I promised to get in touch with her to find out. I really couldn't see Vinny in a law office doing a boring job for low pay.

I did send Keesha a WhatsApp and she took a while to respond. She said that her agent found her acting jobs and communicated with PR agencies on her behalf. She did not do any of this personally. However, she said that it was great that I had got in touch and were we ready for the party on New Years Eve? I said I couldn't wait and that we had booked flights and a hotel and were looking forward to seeing her again. I asked how Barry was? She said that they were seeing a lot of each other, and she felt that this could be love this time. He was everything she wanted in a man. Kind, caring and also made her laugh. I hoped that it would work out for her.

Afterwards, I thought about Kevin and how good I had felt helping him. I had felt some sense of independence and also interested in the research he was doing. I knew I wanted to have a career of my own. I really needed to go back to college to complete my degree. I still wasn't sure what I wanted to study but I started to look at small liberal arts colleges in the Northeast.

Chapter 11

A very merry Christmas....

In the middle of December, a strike was announced at the State University. The strike would be held during the last week of term disrupting some of the exams to be held that week. This strike was discussed on the Jerry Levens' commuter show with callers being very divided about whether it was in the interests of the students.

On December 17 the Mayor held his first Charity Ball and this was a huge success. It was a glamorous, well-attended event. Immediately after the Ball, the Mayor announced his intention to make the Ball an annual event. Next year, it was intended to invite an A list celebrity to host the event.

There was much speculation by Jerry Levens on his radio show which extended to people calling in as to who this celebrity might be. The city did not have many famous residents. There was a player who had played NFL for the Las Vegas Raiders before he retired and who now lived in the Southern Hills. People struggled to think of anyone else. There was, of course, Keesha Miles, who was an actor in a popular soap opera. She had come this year and had taken part in the Charity Ball. Otherwise not many people that could be classed as "A" list..

People suggested local businesspeople who had been very successful could be chosen. Someone recommended asking the priest from the Catholic Church in downtown.

In the national news the "Harry and Meghan" documentary had high viewing figures on Netflix, but very poor reviews from the public. A look at Rotten Tomatoes showed that it received 45% from critics and only 19% from the public. Reviews in the British Press were, as expected, harsh. *The Guardian*, a left leaning British publication, described the arrival of the documentary.

"dropping like a turd into a stocking, may be the royal family's feeling – but for the rest of us it is entertainment, and indeed an education of sorts."

The BBC said in an article dated 9 December 2022 about Volume 1, the first three episodes,

"If you watched the trailers and thought, Harry and Meghan, Netflix's heavily promoted series, was going to be explosive, prepare to be disappointed.........To put it kindly this is slow-burn television."

The BBC say there were a lot of teasers, but not many real revelations.

The Independent newspaper reporting on the second volume of the docuseries, and referring to the wealth and privilege surrounding the Royal Family, said on Thursday 15 December:

"After three more episodes, covering the royal wedding up to their exit (which they, insufferably, describe as their "freedom flight") I felt sad and a bit grumpy. It's not nice to have people telling you how hard their lives are non-stop for three hours, particularly on the same day that nurses have been forced to hold their biggest strike in UK history as they fight for better pay."

In the UK there were articles on the Duke and Duchess every day in the Press and many comments on the documentary by members of the public. The release of the documentary was followed by a brief respite and then it was announced that Prince Harry was to release his memoir "Spare". Some may have felt that this was over exposure of the Duke and Duchess in the festive season.

Jinni - a happy time....

When I look back on December 2022, I feel warm inside – I was so happy during that month. I put a new advert onto the internet for Christmas nails and we were booked up until Christmas Eve.

We painted nails in greens and reds which were the favourite colours and we did some fantastic gel nail designs.

On December 17th I went to the Mayor's Charity Ball. I took my three closest friends with me. I had bought a Tory Burch dress and I wore my hair up, and my mother's diamond necklace. I had never felt so glamorous. Song came round to my apartment to help me get ready. I had the most relaxing bath and massage. Song then did my makeup and nails.

I felt like a million dollars walking into the Hilton Hotel ballroom with my friends. Waiters were on hand with glasses of bubbly for everyone. I could see many of my customers at the event including Janine who read out the results of the silent auction. The dinner was good to say it had been produced for so many people. After dinner and the auction, I got up and danced to the band. What a wonderful evening. To top it all when I got home Song was waiting for me.

Song and I spent many hours together during December. She was so beautiful and loving and would give me massages or comb my hair or paint my nails. I loved being fussed over – such a difference from my salon where I fussed over customers every day.

After the mayor's ball a woman rang to make an appointment at the salon and requested that I do her nails. It turned out that she was the mother of Vinny, Amara's friend. She said her name was Joan. She wanted to ask me about Amara. I explained that Amara was my niece and I called her over to say hello. I could sense from Amara's body language that this was not someone she liked or felt comfortable with.

"Hello Amara" she said "I was just asking your aunt how happy you are working here. If it is going to be a permanent thing."

Amara said that she was working in the salon until she went back to school in the next academic year. She also said that she knew Vinny was going to Washington DC to study for a Certificate to be a paralegal.in January.

Joan nodded "It is really important that Vinny starts to develop a sense of self" she said "He needs to start working towards being independent and not reliant on his father and I. I hope that you are happy for him to go to Washington."

I felt this was all highly inappropriate and I was pleased that Amara was polite and agreed with her. I was also happy when Joan left the salon, although I would always do her nails if she booked and paid.

When I got a spare minute later, I asked to speak to Amara in the back room. I had no idea until then how mixed up she was. I knew that I should have spoken to her earlier about going back to school, but this was hard to do without her losing face. However, with her father leaving her and Barb and all the issues around that, plus her friend being sent away to Washington DC to college, it seemed that she had a lot of problems.

She seemed to want to go to college but really didn't have a clear view of what to do.

That evening I spoke to my niece Arpa in Thailand, and we talked about Somchai and his family. Arpa said that she did not understand what it must be like to live in America. It seemed to her that we have freedoms in the US and the ability to do so much, but also people can be overwhelmed by opportunities and become lost. She felt Amara was a lost soul.

I wondered what we could do to help Amara.

Arpa wondered if it would do Amara good to live in a different culture for a while.

"Does she know anything about our culture in Thailand?" she asked.

I didn't really know, but I assumed not. She had grown up very influenced by her mother and American culture I said.

Arpa said that there were programs for American or European students to come to Bangkok to volunteer at an orphanage. The volunteers worked with the children helping them with sports and some education classes. Students didn't have to know the Thai language as the children were taught in English. The orphanage didn't have a lot of funds so full-time paid staff were few. They relied on volunteers to help with the children.

I thought this sounded like a really good idea. The exposure to a different culture would be very stimulating for a young person who seemed to have lost their way.

I promised I would mention this to Amara, and I did the next day.

Amara was intrigued by the idea of living in Bangkok for a while. Also, she loved children and the idea of working with children was very appealing to her. She said she would think about it over the Christmas break.

Somchai and Randi came to see me over the Christmas break and I cooked for them. They seemed happy and in love.

It was a lovely time and I want to hold that memory in my heart. I didn't know then how things would change in January....

Ellie - determined to make her voice heard....

When the strike was announced I immediately volunteered to be on the picket line. I was told that I should join the people picketing the south entrance to the University campus. This was the entrance that Kevin and I often used.

Kevin was not going to come out on strike. He did not approve of the strike; he told me for the umpteenth time. He had a good salary and opportunities at the University and did not feel the need to shake the status quo.

"What about me?" I asked "do you not care about my prospects? You know that I am paid per course I teach and as has happened this term, my hours can be cut at short notice."

It was then that he dropped the bombshell he said, "But how can you expect to have any prospects, Ellie?" he looked me in the eye "You don't even have the minimum needed for a career in higher education. You dropped out of the PhD you were enrolled in while we were in England, remember? You may be able to get some teaching with a master's degree. But here or in England you will never progress without a doctorate."

I stared at him as I couldn't believe he was talking like this "Yet you knew this, Kevin" I said "You were quite happy for me to support you while you studied. You never queried why I gave up my doctoral studies. In fact, we were happy and comfortable living in England. It is only here that my qualifications are an issue."

I was starting to get really angry "Why did you insist we come here if you knew that I didn't have the minimum qualifications to get a permanent position teaching? You must have known that before we came. I know you wanted to be near your mom, but it seems you quite forgot me or the impact this decision would have on me."

By now we were squaring up to each other and shouting.

Kevin said "I guess I knew you would never stick at anything long enough to achieve anything. You never finished your doctorate. Also, look at you"

He eyed me up and down "Let's be honest. You are fat, Ellie, and yet you can't stick going to the gym to work out and get in shape. It's the story of your life – anything for a nice, easy life."

He was going red in the face and carried on shouting "but take something which anybody with half a brain would avoid and you are there. Speaking out about a mugging on the radio, YouTube videos on fat shaming and now the British Royal Family. All designed to provoke comments – but for what purpose? Where are you going with it? It is all pointless. You can rant on all you like about the rights of fat people, but people will always find fat people unattractive and carry on just the same."

I interrupted him here "Oh my word, Kevin" I said "I never knew you were such a misogynist. Women should not have to be defined by their bodies or how men see them".

Kevin went on "For goodness sake listen to yourself. Fat is not a feminist issue; it is a health issue and also goddam unattractive. Then your other cause. Two rich privileged people ranting on about ill-treatment from the British Royal Family. They left the

UK and are prepared to tell everything for a huge sum of money on Netflix. I can only begin to imagine how rich they are getting from people like you following them. Best way to address their complaints is to ignore them and what you will find is if we all do that they will cease to be relevant. But you, you must wade into the debate. Is that a sign of someone intelligent? It seems moronic to me.

Also, I know you use a pseudonym when you make YouTube videos -but this is pointless as you show your face and anyone who knows us will know it is you. This includes your students and our colleagues at the University. When you go on Facebook you use your own name. You haven't the sense to make up a name. Yet it seems to me almost everyone else who writes seem to use made up names. The internet is an evil place, and if you know what is good for you then you should avoid it. You are posting comments about people you have never met and know nothing about.

What on earth my colleagues would think if they find out you are taking part in a stupid debate that is little better than a soap opera is horrifying to me. You need to take a long hard look at yourself".

He turned on his heel and stormed out of the house. It was a very serious row and he had hurt me deeply with his comments. I was shaking and in tears. I laid on the couch sobbing. How could he talk to me like that?

I never realised he felt like that. "Fat is unattractive" – he had said. Did he find me unattractive now? At one time, we couldn't keep our hands off each other. He used to lust after me, now he thinks I am unattractive, I sobbed.

The issues with Harry and Meghan are part of history. I reasoned. Why should I not want to be involved in the debate? I agreed with Kevin they were both rich and privileged. However, they had a number of complaints against the British Press for privacy intrusion and there were also accusations of structural racism and mental health issues while living as part of the British Royal Family.

After feeling hurt and upset, I began to get angry. As a lecturer, students listened when I spoke, and I enjoyed that attention. I was an intelligent woman, and someone needed to speak up about the issues I was discussing.

I really resented Kevin's comments – "if you had half a brain" he had said. How dare he! I had studied hard to get my master's degree. I had a master's degree in business management. I had worked for years now as a university lecturer. "I supported YOU Kevin!" I shouted out loud even though I was on my own. I had worked while Kevin studied for his doctorate. I had not resented the fact as I loved him and wanted him to do well. But I thought we were a team. I thought he appreciated me. Perhaps I should have married a rich man who would not have expected me to work and who would have looked after me. " You, never looked after me did you Kevin?" I was alone but shouting out loud. "You said we were equals. You didn't want a woman who relied on you – you wanted a soul mate, an equal".

Yet when we came to America, Kevin had (in my mind) abandoned me while he pursued his own career. There had not even been a discussion about how I could earn more. I was just ignored while he pursued his career. This was despite us having money worries. Yes, I know Jenni helped us out all the time, but this was not like having our own money.

And Meghan Markle thought she had complaints? Living in a mansion with streaming stations throwing money at her and Prince Harry. Deep down I knew that she probably had to come up with something sensational and complain and whinge about Harry's family to justify the money from the streaming companies. But at the moment I was not thinking logically. I was FURIOUS.

Then I got to thinking about his fat comments. Again, how dare he? He was a big man himself until very recently when he started going to the gym. Who is he to judge me? Also, without being crude he always loved my large breasts, or so I thought.

In the midst of all this anger I decided to make another YouTube video. But this time I would speak out bluntly about the "Harry and Meghan" docuseries on Netflix. Believe me, I did not hold back. I said things that probably were best kept to myself. I called her a gold digger and him a spoiled whinging child. I talked about their rich, privileged lifestyle and the way they flaunted that while complaining about how difficult life was. I quoted from the *Independent* newspaper about how difficult it was to listen to them when there was a nurses strike in the UK and (of course) I mentioned our own strike at the State University. I should have stopped there, but I didn't I really got carried away ranting on and called them a lot of names and wished them bad luck.

I took out all my anger on two people I had never met (and was never likely to meet) and posted it online for anybody to read. It attracted a lot of views and suddenly I had all the attention I craved. Of course, it also attracted trolls. These were people who put messages on about what a sad, disgusting person I was and wished all sorts of bad things would happen to me.

I had the attention I craved now – but how to follow it up? But was what I did to get the attention really sad and disgusting? I didn't feel good about it, but it was done in a moment of anger, and it was too late to retract it.

In the days following the row Kevin and I hardly spoke. We were just about speaking when I took part in the picket line on the last week of term. Perhaps I should have given more attention to losing weight, but I was stubborn and instead gave more attention to my activist activities.

During the strike week I was surprised when Kevin told me about the possibility of some teaching in the new year. Peter, a colleague of his, lived with a woman, Maureen Neves, who was the administrator at The Palmer Institute, a small private college about 50 miles from here. Due to unforeseen circumstances, they needed someone at short notice to teach a couple of Statistics classes in the new term. I immediately sent my resume with a covering letter. This teaching would make up for the shortfall at the State University.

It was only when we went to Jenni's for Christmas dinner that Kevin and I began to talk normally again. Looking at him across the dinner table I felt sick wondering what the future would hold. All I could hear in my head was him saying "fat is unattractive" and wondering if he still loved me and had the hots for me. Also, if I should let anyone speak to me in the way he had and still live with them. I wondered if I had zero self-respect……

Janine - embracing the healthy lifestyle….

In December I put the finishing touches to the mural on the wall of the Institute for the Blind and Visually Impaired. The tactile piece that accompanied it had actually taken me longer than the large mural. However, I was pleased with it, as it was an accurate representation of the two artistes in the main mural. It showed their upper bodies and hands playing their pianos. It was an exciting moment. The Institute was to be officially opened by the Mayor on 2 January and I was invited to the event where we would also officially unveil the mural.

I was also working with the Mayor's office and was due to announce the results of the Silent Auction at the Charity Ball. The Ball was a very glamorous occasion, and I enjoyed every minute of it. I wore a column dress from Proenza Schouler and strappy heels. I wore my hair up and had my nails and make-up done in the afternoon. There was a photo of the mural at the Mayor's Ball and also the tactile picture. The Mayor talked about the mural and the tactile piece during his speech. I noticed that afterwards a couple of blind people who were attending the Ball went over and touched the tactile piece. I went over to them to ask them what they thought. They were very complimentary saying that it helped them to enjoy art and they thanked me for doing it. It was a great evening and I liked the way the Mayor was taking the City. He was ambitious and intended to put it onto the map.

We were hoping to move into our new home before the end of the year and I was also excited about that. It was a very happy and optimistic time.

Although it was the run up to Christmas we continued with the running and eating healthily. Granny made pasta with chicken but this time she cooked it with a healthier sauce and invited Amy and I over to eat with her. Amy seemed a bit down when she arrived. It turned out she had had a big argument with a friend of hers about running. Her friend had told her that she was dicing with death running at her age. She was too old, and it would kill her! Granny told her that that was rubbish as her doctor had told her it was perfectly safe. Amy had told her friend this and her friend had replied that Amy's doctor did not know what he was talking about. She said she knew someone who had gone out running and had a massive heart attack and dropped dead. I could see that this type of negative talk would be very upsetting for Amy. I thought she was looking well, and I asked if she had lost weight with all the running we had been doing? Granny brought the scales out and Amy was thrilled to see she had lost 4 pounds. Eating the pasta and talking about weight loss cheered her up – although she said she would probably put all the weight back on over Christmas!

I suggested that a way to cheer us up would be to buy some workout clothes. After eating and before running we called in at the mall and looked at exercise wear. This provoked a lot of laughing as Granny and Amy could not see themselves in some of the outfits which they felt were designed for 18-year-olds. They had previously been to Goodwill and bought T-shirts and leggings to work out in. On cool evenings they wore these with a knitted bobble hat and training shoes they had had for years. After a lot of humming and hahing and saying they could not afford it – they eventually picked out some firm support high waisted 7/8 leggings and sport bras and T-shirts. They looked great. I could not believe these were women in their 70s when they tried on their new exercise wear. They looked more like they were in their 50s. I felt we were making really good progress.

It was now quite cold in the evening – but we did not notice this as we did our 25 minutes of running and walking! We were making progress. I was sure we would all be running a 5k in 2023.

Our Christmas was quiet and after we had eaten we sat in front of the fire with a glass of wine and toasted our new home and all that 2023 held in store for us.....

Recipe for healthier chicken pasta

Eating a healthier diet does not have to mean missing out on flavour, so this recipe for spicy chicken includes lots of tasty components.

Ingredients

1 or 2 tablespoons of a neutrally flavoured oil, such as rapeseed oil, known in the USA as canola oil.

2 tablespoons each of the following:

Grated ginger

Chopped garlic.

2 birds eye chillis, seeds removed, chopped

3 or 4 spring onions separated into white and green parts, sliced into rounds.

1 tablespoon of tomato paste

1 can of chopped tomatoes or tomato passata, depending upon how smooth you want the finished dish to be.

200 grammes of diced chicken, either skinless boneless thighs or breast meat.

Method:

Heat the oil to medium for a few seconds and then add the ginger, garlic and chopped pepper, plus the white rounds of spring onion.

Stir the mixture constantly over a medium heat until fragrant and the spring onion rounds are beginning to soften. Do not allow the mixture to stick or burn.

Once the mixture is ready, add the diced chicken, distributing around the pan and stirring until the outside of the chicken has turned white. Increase the heat a little to speed up the cooking at this stage. Do not allow the chicken to get too brown, as the cooking process will continue in the next stage.

Stir in the tomato paste and cook for a minute, to reduce any bitterness.

Add the chopped tomatoes or passata and stir into the mixture. Bring it to the boil briefly and then turn the heat down to simmer.

Continue to simmer for 10 to 15 minutes, depending upon how big the chicken dice are.

Test the flavour and if it is a little bitter, add up to a teaspoonful of sugar. You might want to add a few grinds of black pepper at this point.

Serve with rice and top with some of the green leaves of the spring onion.

Amara - a brighter day....

In December I finished the interviewing for the research project and wrote up my results. There was a strike at the State University, so I agreed to meet Kevin in a coffee shop again. We sat together in a booth and went over the results together. I loved the way he had respect for my views and listened to me. He always answered my questions thoughtfully. I wondered what it would be like to be in a relationship with such an intellectual man. I was sorry that the project had ended as I wanted to do more for Kevin. Perhaps he had the same idea as he mentioned there may be some more work on the research project when he had consulted with his colleague Dr John Strickland in Georgia.

I was surprised when Jinni brought up the idea about me living in Thailand for a few months and volunteering at an orphanage. Although I wouldn't be paid for my work at the orphanage, I could stay there, and they would feed me so I didn't have to pay out much myself. Plus, I had relatives I did not know who lived in Bangkok who wanted to meet me and take me out on my days off. At first, I thought – no way. But as I mulled it over, it became more and more attractive. I saw myself as 100% American, but to live in a different culture and find out about my dad's family would be so interesting. Also, to learn a few words of the Thai language would be fun and I could talk to dad and Auntie Jinni when I came back and surprise them. It would also look good on an application to university. I had not dared mention it to mom yet as she might go through the roof if I was to leave her as well! It was just a possibility.

I saw on social media that my friends from high school were returning from university and a few were meeting up at the "Albion" a night club in downtown. I decided it might be fun to swallow my pride and face them. So far since quitting university I had laid low. I didn't want questions about why I had dropped out of university and what was I doing now. I planned on what I would say if anyone asked. I could say I was spending a gap year in Thailand starting in January and then going to a small liberal arts college in the North East. I didn't intend to mention the nail salon. Vinny had something else on that evening, so I went on my own.

As it turned out my friends were just pleased to see me, and no-one asked what I was doing. In fact, they were too busy talking about themselves! I did feel slightly envious hearing about how well some of them were doing, but I told myself that my time would come.

The Albion was packed and as the night wore on, we started downing cocktails and chasers. Near to midnight we got up on the dance floor. I couldn't believe who I saw on the other side of the room. I thought my eyes were deceiving me. It looked like Kevin and a couple of other men with a group of people about my age.

I had had a few drinks by then, so I was not as shy as normal. I went over and spoke to him. It turned out that the post graduate students in Kevin's class were having a Christmas drinks party and they had invited a few of the professors to join them.

"Come and dance" I said, and to my surprise he did. I was so happy dancing with him and then we sat and had another drink or two. By then, the room was starting to go round. Kevin said he would arrange for me a Uber. Although I lived completely across town from him, he insisted on going with me in the Uber. I cuddled up to him in the back seat and we kissed and held each other.

In the morning when I woke up, I had a crushing hangover. Plus, I wondered what had happened last night. Was it just a dream or did I really kiss and fondle professor Kevin in the back of an Uber? I thought about his wife. A customer at the nail salon who had always been friendly to me. She had asked me to join her for a coffee after I had finished work. I think she also teaches at the State University. I also remembered how respectful and kind he had been while I worked on the research project. He had even talked about more work. A sinking feeling in the pit of my stomach told me that I had most probably ruined that now. However, why did he insist on getting in the Uber with me? Surely it was his fault as I lived the other side of the city to him and there was no need for him to go with me. Perhaps he thought I was drunk, and he wanted to protect me. Yet was it protecting me, holding me and kissing me?

And on and on and on my thoughts went – twisting and twirling in my head. What a fool I had been. I pulled the covers over my head. I must be the most mixed-up person in the whole of the USA. The thought of Thailand seemed more and more appealing……

Chapter 13

The start of a new year...

The year ended on a high in the City with the downtown looking festive decorated by the City Council. The Walks shopping area looked especially beautiful decorated with lights and poinsettias. On New Year's Eve the Mayor held a countdown to midnight outside the City Hall with fireworks at midnight. This was broadcast on the local TV station and also many people came in person to the downtown. The Mayor said he was looking forward to the best year ever in 2023.

In other parts of the city there were still some issues. The strike at the State University was not resolved. The Union resolved to strike again in the second week of the new term in the new year.

In Gent Town the homeless population had taken over a couple of vacant lots and also the area beneath the metro line at the station. Commuters had to pass through this area to get onto the trains and were often stopped and asked for money. There were also a couple of violent incidents, with one woman being threatened with a knife.

Jerry Levens kept the news topical throughout the holiday season and reported on the issues with the Strike and the reputed violence around the metro station.

One person calling in who asked to remain anonymous said this was all linked to a number of illegal immigrants that had moved to the city in recent months. This person stated that there was an underground website that told people cities in the US to go to where they would not be harassed by Immigration Officials and this City had featured on the website in the fall. As a result, that had been an influx of undocumented aliens.

Jerry Levens was interested to know more about this theory. Jerry said that the city was not a border city and that issues with undocumented aliens had not been reported previously.

Another person rang in who also asked for anonymity and this person said that these people were Chinese and had come into America across the southern border and moved to the city as a result of information they had found on the internet.

This was a new topic for the City and Jerry Levens asked his assistant Libby to find out more after the call in.

In wider events the "Harry and Meghan" documentary was still in the news   Also, there were announcements that Prince Harry's memoir "Spare" was to be released on January 10, 2023. The book was also to be available on audio books and Harry was to narrate the audio version. The book had been ghost written by J P Moehringer. The publicity stated

"For Harry this is his story at last.   With its raw, unflinching honesty Spare is a landmark publication full of insight, revelation, self-examination, and hard-won wisdom about the eternal power of love over grief."

Prince Harry also announced that he would donate his proceeds from Spare to various charities including $1,500,000 to Sentebale, an organisation which supported children and young people in Lesotho and Botswana affected by HIV/Aids. He also promised £500,000 to WellChild.

Jinni - becomes closer to Song.....

The new year began on a high note – my accountant sent me the results for the 2022 financial year, and they were the best I had ever seen for my business. The salon was profitable, and I knew I could (and should) be able to afford expanding into the new regeneration district. This made me very happy. When I had arrived in the city, my marriage had broken down, and I had only my divorce settlement to help me get started on my own. I felt confident that investing the money in the salon had been a good move and I felt that good times were ahead.

I also looked at Song, as she filed nails across the salon and could not believe how lucky I was to have her in my life. She was so beautiful. Also, so loving and caring. I felt like the most beautiful woman in the world when I was in her arms, and I hope I made her feel the same way too. I was much older than her, but the age difference didn't seem to matter when we were together. We spent hours talking about growing up she in China and me in Thailand. She told me about Guangzhou, the city she grew up in.

She was an only child, in line with China's laws at the time. But her memories were always blighted by the pressure her father put on her to perform academically. She had always loved doing her make-up and hair and nails and reading about female celebrities who were famous for their beauty. She idolised women who were American celebrities and had tried to emulate their looks. A favourite of hers was the Kardashian family. She had been able to see their show on cable TV when her father was out. In the Garden Hotel (a 5 star hotel in downtown Guangzhou) there was a band that played in the evening and the Chinese lady who sang with them had had her figure enhanced to look like Kim Kardashian from the rear. Song and her friend had sneaked into the hotel to watch her sing and at the break had asked how she had achieved the look. She was very haughty and did not want to talk to them, at first. However, she had admitted she had been to the USA and had the work done there by a plastic surgeon. Song said that was when her dreams of America started. She imagined herself living in a a gated mansion with her personal maid and having "work" done to enhance her body. Also, a friend of a friend who was older than her and had a very rich father had gone to Los Angeles to study. She had had a wonderful time and had lived in Palos Verdes, which was south of the downtown. She had taken her maid with her. She drove a Mercedes to the University of Southern California (USC) where she was a student. She had been invited to many parties and had found Americans very outgoing and friendly.

Meanwhile Song found it difficult to get interested in the academic books her father brought home for her to read. Her record at school had always been mediocre and she felt she was the biggest disappointment to her family. Her father expected so much, and she delivered so little. She struggled so much. When her father suggested she go to America on an academic scholarship she saw it as a chance to achieve her dreams. However, the truth had been brutal. She didn't get into USC as her grades were not good enough. Instead, she was accepted at a small college in an area of Los Angeles called the San Fernando Valley. When she had arrived she had nowhere to live. She had gone with a friend to look for accommodation and had been horrified to find out the cost of renting an apartment. Very quickly, she found out that Los Angeles was a such an expensive city and she had no chance of the lifestyle she had dreamed about while watching the Kardashians on TV. Instead, she ended up living in a tiny walk up apartment and having to clean houses to make ends meet.

She is such a child, I thought, and one that has been cruelly used by her father. Not everyone is clever and academic. Just because he is clever and academic does not mean his daughter would be the same. I wanted to give her the happiness she deserved and had been so missing from her family life. I told her that working in the salon with me she would never have to study academic books again.

That was my dream – for Song to be happy. Yes, I was worried when illegal workers were mentioned on the Jerry Levens show and also when the topic came up in the salon. But I was in love now, and I would defend Song to the end.

Song had started to spend a lot of time at my apartment as we discovered more about each other. I loved her so much. Perhaps my love for her made her want to open up and be honest about her time in Los Angeles. She had cleaned homes in the Hollywood Hills. These homes were owned she believed by media types and minor celebrities. Seeing the wealth and lifestyle they enjoyed she felt that she deserved some nice things too. She had taken smallish things while cleaning. A tub of bronzer, a bottle of nail polish, things rich people wouldn't notice had gone. Her friend, Lily, had been on the take. She took more expensive things. Song had cautioned her to be careful. However, Lily wanted the gowns and jewels she saw in these homes. Lily couldn't believe how careless these people were with their wealth.

I expect I knew what was coming. Lily and Song had worked as a duo cleaning. One day the manager of the cleaning company called them in. There had been a complaint from one of the houses they cleaned. The lady said that a Cartier watch had gone missing, and she blamed the cleaners as there had not been a break-in. It was a house they cleaned and they could not prove they had not taken the watch so of course, they were let go from their jobs. The owner of the cleaning company told them that she would not be turning them over to the police as they were not supposed to be working in the USA. He said he would be in a lot of trouble also if the police reported him to the immigration authorities. However, he wasn't going to pay them the money he owed them. Although relieved they were not being reported to the police the loss of the money was a big blow to them. That coupled with poor grades that meant they might be kicked out of the college was what had caused them to go on to the internet to find somewhere friendly to live.

My poor darling, I thought. Life has been so cruel to her. A domineering, overbearing father and now a set-up at the cleaning company. I was absolutely sure Song would not have taken a valuable watch. Maybe little things that seemed harmless, but she would never be so immoral or foolish.

Yes, I was in love in early January, and I could not get enough of Song.

In my own family Somchai told me that he felt it would be the best thing ever for Amara to live in Thailand for a while. He would love it if she got to know his family, and something about the Thai culture. Amara seemed to be coming round to the idea.

Barb had not been to the salon since the evening she came demanding to know where Somchai was. I knew from Amara that she was finding it difficult to manage money since Somchai had left. Money was in short supply. But I asked myself why would you pay to go to Keesha's party if you were really short of money? Taking a flight and staying at the Marriott. Surely that money should have been spent on something more important, such as a utility bill. I would never understand Barb in a million years.

I was glad Somchai seemed happier with Randi. Randi seemed to be less materialistic than Barb. I would not have wanted to live in their apartment in that part of the city, but they seemed happy there.

It just proves that money can't buy love – I said to myself – Somchai is happier than he has ever been now he is living in Gent Town in a tiny apartment. He doesn't care that he doesn't live in a mansion in the Southern Hills anymore. He just wants to be with the woman he loves. In my mind this was so romantic.....

Ellie - a rude awakening....

On December 27 I received an email from the Union to say that despite the Strike management had not accepted our demands. There was to be another Strike in the second week of term in the new year.

I wondered what had happened to my application for teaching at the Palmer Institute as I scrolled through my emails and text messages, but I could not see anything other than an acknowledgement. I mentioned this to Kevin, who said he would follow up with his colleague. I was more than qualified for the position, which was teaching first year undergraduate students, and willing to step in on very short notice so I was surprised I had not heard anything.

I noticed that there were a lot of comments on my latest YouTube videos about the "Harry and Meghan" documentary. Some agreed with me and said they felt I had done the right thing speaking up. However, others were, in my opinion, downright rude. I was accused of being racist and a "Karen". I did not know, initially, what a Karen was. So I looked it up on the internet, *Wikipedia* said it was a slang term for

"a middle-class white woman who is perceived as entitled or demanding beyond the scope of what is normal"

I felt disrespected by the use of this term to describe me. I then became even more angry and wrote a quick reply saying that it was okay to disagree with me, but I felt I should be treated with respect. This provoked even more angry comments. I went back and forth starting with a couple of people that soon grew to about 10 people. After about half an hour we were trading insults. I was shaking and visibly upset. I decided to take a break and went to make a cup of coffee. In the kitchen I tried to calm down by taking deep breaths and pacing around. Thankfully I decided to go out and do some grocery shopping rather than look at the comments again that day.

A couple of days later Kevin got a call on his phone early and went to his study to take it. I got out of bed and started making breakfast. When he came into the kitchen, his face looked like thunder.

"You haven't got an interview for the position at the Palmer Institute, Ellie" he said, "I asked yesterday if my colleague could check your application when I mentioned you hadn't heard anything. She just rang back to say it is correct that you have not been short listed for an interview. She should not have done this and only did it as a favour to me. So this is very unofficial. Nothing is on the record, but bottom line is you won't be working there."

I was quite shocked "But I was going to help them out – by taking over a course at short notice. Why would they not want me?"

"Ellie, nothing has officially been said. But I can see why they might not want you. Yes, you have qualifications and can competently teach the class, but look at your online presence."

"Pardon" I said genuinely shocked. What was he talking about? "I record all my YouTube videos under a pseudonym, so I am always completely anonymous".

"Anonymous" Kevin snorted "Is that what you think? It is very easy to go onto the internet and make a little video and bad-mouth people with no evidence. This is especially true if you think you are anonymous. But remember, you are on the video, Ellie, I have seen it, talking about the Royals. You certainly didn't do anything to disguise your face. Anybody who had seen a picture of you would know it was you."

"Then there is the issue of arguments. Especially if people post that they don't like your video. But this is all very public, and you don't know who is looking at this. If I was making hiring decisions, I would be very wary of employing someone to be around students who did things like that. Getting into slanging matches with others about alleged racism."

He was really fired up now: "I warned you about going onto the internet and making your views known. It seems looking at your latest video that you put forward very controversial remarks without any evidence other than how it made you feel. You then got into arguments with people who commented and traded insults. I know you posted your video under the name "opinionated limey" but my understanding is that it is possible to trace the name of the person who posted the video unless that person has been clever and put in place certain privacy options. I expect you didn't know that and have not made sure your true identity remained private. In my opinion you have not considered your online image and it may be and note I am saying "may be" because I don't really know. It may be that the Palmer Institute are worried about having such a person teaching a class for them."

I felt sick – Kevin always made some sort of sense when he talked, no matter how frustrating it could be. It is easy to say that we all have the right to speak up and what I put on the internet was not related to what I teach. However, I could see what he was saying. My desire to be listened to on social media had made me somewhat controversial.

Later, I went onto the internet and found out from Monster.com that a study found that 67% of employers screen job candidates through social networks. The same study found that 54% of applicants were disqualified after viewing an applicant's social media. A company called Proactivepersonnel.net said that employers might check your social profile to find out if you engage in negative behaviours like racism or excessive swearing. I could see how the YouTube video and subsequent conversation would cause red flags to an employer worried about this. I noted that Proactivepersonnel.net had recommended responding to comments professionally and respectfully. The whole interaction yesterday with people who had called me a Karen had NOT been either professional or respectful.

So I had to agree reluctantly with Kevin – I had been too impulsive and it was very likely my YouTube video and comments that had stopped me getting even an interview for the work, although of course we had no evidence that this was the case. I just had not been short-listed without a reason given.

We now had to face January with a loss of my earnings at the State University. Plus, even if the Union won I wondered if I would gain anything? Maybe the State University were also looking at my online profile.

We had some money from the Insurance Company for the theft of the ring and I knew Jenni would never see us starve. However, what were we going to do in the long run? Had I effectively spoiled my chances of any more teaching?

I really didn't want to meet Jenni at the nail salon as planned but I did not know how I could get out of it.

There was a big conversation in the nail salon about the Jerry Levens show that morning.

"I can't believe there are undocumented workers in this city" Jenni said "and Chinese too. It seems far-fetched."

She seemed to ignore Song who was giving her a pedicure at the time. I am sure she is Chinese. I wondered if she had papers? She seemed to be keeping out of the discussion. She was a beautiful, young girl with long glossy hair to her waist and so slim.

Jinni, who I had found out was very adept at these things, turned the conversation to other things. The Mayor's firework display on New Year's Eve – were any of us going to go?

I was relieved there was no mention of Harry and Meghan or my YouTube video in the salon. As we left Jenni asked if I would like to go for a coffee.

How could I say no? In the coffee shop Jenni mentioned that Kevin had mentioned that I had been posting videos on the Royal Family on YouTube. So she had watched the video and read the comments. She said it was not her place to interfere. Inwardly I sighed as I knew she was going to interfere anyway. However, she said, she would advise keeping out of discussions like that. She understood I might be a little homesick and want to think about good old Blighty and the Royal Family, but she felt there were other ways to satisfy this. She said there were groups of British expats who met up and got to chat about the old country. There were not groups within this city as far as she could see, but why didn't I form one? I could advertise in *the Pinnacle* or on the radio for other Brits to meet for coffee perhaps once a month and it could go from there?

I wanted to be an activist and be listened to and she was suggesting I form a social group? It seemed farfetched at the time. However, I told her it was a good idea and I would think about it.

It was a good idea, but would it help me raise my profile as I desired? Had what I had done so far helped raise my profile or lower it as was suggested?

By New Year's Eve I was depressed and not really looking forward to 2023. I could not see a way out of my troubles. We went to a party at a neighbour's home. As we toasted the new year, I felt that Kevin and I had drifted further and further away from each other and I had messed up all our chances of a bright future in the USA

Janine - the mural is unveiled...

At the beginning of January my mural on the wall of the Institute for the Blind and Visually Impaired was unveiled. There was a ceremony with the Mayor and the President of the Institute present. I was pleased that a crowd of people had gathered, including Gene and my Granny and Amy. The local TV station was also there and the newspaper *the Pinnacle*.

The Institute had invited a few of their new students to the unveiling. They were invited to come over and touch the tactile art. I could see them running their hands over the plaster painting and feeling the faces and hands of the musicians. I could see how much pleasure they got out of being able to enjoy art this way.

Although the day went well, the following day reading reactions to the mural in the local paper I was disappointed that they were mixed. This is despite me taking part in a radio phone-in on the topic of the mural.

"What do these two artistes have to do with either this City or the Institute?" people asked.

"Surely we have some people in this City who are blind and have distinguished themselves who could have featured in the mural" someone else commented.

"The Institute is not a music school so why musicians?" was another comment. Other people loved the idea of blind musicians on the wall of the Institute even though they were not personally connected with the Institute.

"Perhaps Stevie will come and give us a concert" said one person "he is an inspiration to blind people everywhere."

Nevertheless, I was pleased with the mural and the *Pinnacle* described it as "inspiring". They had sent a copy of the article to Stevie Wonder for his comments.

The day after I got a call when I was at the Cooperative from the Mayor's office. The mayor came on the line.

"Hello Janine" he said "I am really happy with the mural you did at the Institute. The tactile plaster art is also very good, and I saw it was already being appreciated by students of the Institute at the unveiling."

I thanked him and said that I felt Street Art really helped to liven up a downtown district.

He said he agreed, and he asked me to paint another mural, this time on the wall of another building in the regeneration area. "We have just leased this building to a whole foods shop. The new owner, Gary Brinker, has a small area of land he farms where he grows his own produce. The city has let him have the shop at a reduced rate to encourage people in the inner city area to eat healthily and to eat fresh produce. I think a mural on the side of the shop about the fresh produce that he will sell would be great."

I thanked him for the commission and agreed to meet with Gary Brinker to find out more about what he did and what he would like for the mural.

At this time, Gene and I were very busy moving into our new home. At first, we could not get used to the amount of space we had in the new house. It was so beautiful there, filled with light and so spacious.

"I can't wait to fill it with children" Gene said, "how lucky are they going to be, to grow up in a place like this?"

He was now a partner at Alex Gold, and we were financially sound. All we had to do was make a baby. However, that was proving to be not as easy as it sounded. I told myself I was still in my thirties, and we had plenty of time so nothing to worry about yet. If we just went about our daily lives it would happen in good time.

When we first moved in the house and we started to think seriously about bringing a child into the world, I realised how little we knew about children and their upbringing. We were both only children and we had no nieces or nephews. The relatives I keep in touch with were in the main older people. I did not come into contact with children for my job. I had friends that had children, and Gene and I had been to birthday parties and cook outs with friends and their children. But in the main we had little contact with children.

At this time, we went out for a late lunch to a restaurant and pub on the river side just outside of the city. This restaurant had been recommended by a colleague of Gene's as having very good food. When we arrived, we could see that it was very busy. The greeter took us to a table that overlooked the river and a terrace that surrounded the pub. We started to look at the menus. The noise in there was horrendous. There were people talking loudly and laughing, but there were also children running around screaming and shouting. In the middle of the room there was a large table where about 10 people were sat, next to this table was another table where I presume it was their children were sat. The adults were laughing and talking and ordering drinks. The waitress came over with a tray full of beers and wines even though it was only afternoon. They were largely ignoring the children.

The children, who I presume were bored, kept getting up and running around and screaming. No reaction from the main table. Finally, a little child, aged about four, I would guess, went over to the main table. I could hear her talking to her mom and she asked if she could go down to the river. Her mother said she could go if one of the older children went with her. A couple of older children said they would go with her. They then set off out of the restaurant down to the river. I could see the river was flowing rapidly and I could not believe the mother would allow her to go down there.

I looked knowingly at Gene and tried to ask him discreetly what he thought about this. In fact, we were almost shouting to be able to be heard above the din. Gene said he would be worried about the child and would have gone with her to supervise.

We ordered our food then and the noise just got louder as more children got bored and started running around inside the restaurant.

"Why don't you go and look for your sister?" a lady I assumed was the mom said.

A few of the children then went out of the door down to the river. I could see them out of the window. They were playing by the water. It looked muddy and as it was winter it was already starting to grow dark. I began to feel panicky. When were the parents going to check on them? What if one of them fell into the river, the water was flowing fast and they would be swept downstream?

Surely the parents could have kept them amused in the restaurant, if they didn't want to go with them down to the river. Perhaps they could have had games on an ipad? That might have kept them quiet. Shouldn't they have sat at the same table as their children and, actually talked to them instead of to their friends?

I realised then how little I knew about parenting. I couldn't imagine sitting at a table chatting and laughing while my young children were outside playing by the river. I would be panicking and worrying that they were safe. But would that make me an overprotective mom? Weren't moms supposed to give children freedom while at the same time supporting them?

As Gene and I were eating our food the children came running back into the restaurant shouting and screaming. The waitress was just coming over to another table with a food order and followed them. She then slipped on the mud they had left on the floor and nearly went flying!! She managed to stop herself falling at the last minute, but she spilled the food. In the chaos that ensued the parents carried on talking and chatting at their table.

"Oh Daisy look at you" the mother said "you have got mud all over your new shoes." She then turned to her friend "I paid $120 for these and I hope they are not ruined."

A man then started shouting at the older boy who had gone down to the river "What are you doing letting her play in the mud?" he said "you were supposed to be looking after her and look at her"

There seemed a total lack of care about the restaurant and the waitress. By this time there were a few of the waiting staff trying to clean up the mess with mops and a bucket and a brush and shovel.

A man sitting at another table shouted, "Where is our food? We have been waiting for about 40 minutes and that is unacceptable." The waitress apologised and said they would get the food out just as soon as they cleaned the mess up.

To be honest, we were glad to finish our food and leave. In the car on the way home, we couldn't stop talking about the families and their out of control (as we saw it) children. We couldn't believe they would not apologise to the waiting staff for the children tracking mud into the restaurant. We were sure any children we would have would never behave like that.

Just after this Gene read an article about a restaurant in Georgia that had gone viral for imposing an adult surcharge on diners who were unable to control their children's behaviour. This had been reported on several news channels. Comments on social media were divisive with some saying how can the restaurant owner and staff judge what is bad behaviour. It is so subjective to judge behaviour.

I know that you don't need a certificate to prove you can parent before giving birth, but it suddenly seemed like such an enormous responsibility. I felt quite scared about the prospect of bringing a life into the world.

I mentioned this to granny and Amy who said that children are always noisy and boisterous. Amy said she loved going to the Sunday 10 a.m. service at Church as this was the children's service. She said some people had complained that children were running around in the Church and making noise and that was disrespectful. She thought it was lovely. They are the next church members, and we should always welcome them, she felt.

Amy also said, "Jesus said Suffer little children to come unto me, and forbid them not; for of such is the kingdom of God."

I sort of agreed with her. But surely there was no excuse for bad behaviour? I never ran round making noise when I was little in church. Why is it okay for children now to do that?

Granny seemed to agree with Amy about children being allowed to run free and express themselves.

I had so many ideas in my head about what I would do, while at the same time worrying that I would be doing the wrong thing.

Maybe one day we would find out what it was like to be parents. But for now life went on with Gene and I living in our new beautiful home and working hard at our jobs.

In other areas of my life, I was keeping myself very healthy with the exercise I did and the running. We were making progress with the "Couch to 5k". Perhaps progress was slower than it would be if I was on my own due to Amy and Granny being involved. They were getting more active, and it was great to see. Roger, Granny's dog, usually came with us on our runs and even he looked slimmer and fitter than a few months ago. I felt sure we would be able to take part in the city running event planned for March. This involved several races. A marathon for the serious runners. A half marathon, a 10k and a 5k. That was the aim now to take part in that day....

Amara - the project ends and Keesha's party....

At the beginning of January, I went to see Kevin for the last time in his office. My part of the project was completed, and we had a final wash up meeting. It was slightly embarrassing after the incident in the Uber. However, we both acted professionally and as if that evening had never happened. Kevin told me he was very happy with the work I had done, and he felt I should include it in an application to return to university. I explained that I planned to go back to university, but first my aunt had suggested I go to Thailand and work for a few months in an orphanage.

Kevin told me that he thought that was an excellent idea. It would be give me chance to experience a different culture and also to think about what I might want to study when returning to University. He said he would be happy to act as a reference on an application I made.

I felt the meeting went very well and I was coming round to the idea that a few months in Thailand would be very helpful to me.

Vinny left in early January to go to Washington DC. I was sad to see him go, we had grown close and I enjoyed being with him. However, I felt his mother was a force to be reckoned with and he probably had no choice. I promised to visit but it is doubtful if that would ever happen in reality.

I had not mentioned Thailand to mom as I knew she was worried about money as it was. However, despite her money worries she still was excited and went ahead with the trip to Keesha's party. So it was that on New Year's Eve we had caught the flight with Janice to go to Keesha's party. It was an economy flight and absolutely packed. We sat together towards the back and it took the stewardess so long to come around with the cart that we almost missed having drinks before we landed in the big City. The airport in the City was very busy also, but Janice had been before and knew her way around. We caught a taxi to the Marriott and then spent the afternoon in the city looking around. There were some nice shops in the downtown area and we went for a late lunch at an Italian restaurant that served modern Italian cuisine. I had the swordfish with a salad and felt very virtuous. After eating we returned to the Marriott to get ready. Mom and I shared a room and Janice was next door. Mom had bought a new dress and spent ages on her make-up and hair. She looked really nice by the time we were ready. I knew this was a big deal for her and it was nice to see her have some enthusiasm for life again.

We went to Keesha's apartment about 7.30. As we walked over to the apartment, there were quite a few homeless people in the downtown area sleeping in doorways and lying on the sidewalks. We were asked for money on several occasions as we walked along. My heart broke for these people. It was unbearable to think about being in the position where you don't have anywhere to live or people to care about you. We didn't have far to walk as Keesha lived in a nice modern apartment block in the downtown area. There was security on the entrance to the apartment. There was a desk in the lobby and a man greeted us and let us into the area with the elevators. Her apartment was on the 6th floor. I was really impressed when we walked into her apartment as it had a wall of glass and balcony overlooking the city. She had a couple of modular sofas and a glass table and chairs. Her kitchen was open to the main room and looked white and modern. The room was big for an apartment. The views of the City were to die for. It was a beautiful apartment and I wondered, for just a minute, if I had should have been an actress too if it meant you could live like this. Perhaps I had been a bit hasty when I did not want to be a background artiste! Maybe I should have stuck at it and I could be a soap actor now with a beautiful apartment instead of living at home with my mom.

Barry, Keesha's friend, was there and he came over to say Hi. There were also a few other people who were standing around drinking and chatting. Now I am going to have to make a confession. I have never watched "Grangemouth" which is the soap Keesha has a part in! Please don't tell my mom this as she watches it every time it is on. My excuse is I am always busy. Mom and Janice had chatted about the soap on the plane on the way here, so I knew a few things. The head of the clan in the soap was Mary Burton and she was played by an actress who is in her 60s. She is a self-made multi-millionaire with a large house and children who are largely a big disappointment to her. I got a few names while on the plane Wilson, Devon, Keith and Melissa. I had searched the internet for photos of these people so I could recognise them if they were at the party. So far as I could tell the people at the party were not the people I had searched for. I started to chat to a young guy who it turned out worked behind the camera for the show. He seemed really friendly, and we had a few drinks.

Before I knew it, time had flown, and it was about 11 pm and the place was heaving. Music was playing and the door was open to the balcony. I had not seen mom for a while and so I walked out on to the balcony to look for her. There she was. She looked absolutely animated and deeply engrossed in conversation with an older man. I did not recognise the man talking to mom. I guess he would be in his 50s and he had shaved his head.

Mom said "Oh hi Amara".

Turning to her companion she said, "this is Amara, the daughter I was telling you about."

Turning to me she said "let me introduce you to Danny. You know Danny don't you?"

Help! I thought who the heck is he?

"Yes that's right" she blathered on when I didn't immediately answer "this is Danny who plays Gerry, the pastor in the show"

Danny smiled and said "hi Amara, how are you?"

I smiled and said I was having a blast.

I could see mom was in her element chatting to a minor celebrity from the show, so I left them to it.

We all celebrated midnight on the balcony watching the fireworks in the downtown of the city. After midnight, a group of us, including Keesha, decided to go to a bar in the downtown where there was dancing and cocktails. I had lost track of mom and Janice by this time and assumed as they were older that they had gone back to the hotel.

I had a really good night and quite a lot to drink! As it was New Year's Eve we really pushed the boat out! I felt quite drunk by the time I got back to the room about 3 am. All was quiet and dark and there was no sign of mom. If I hadn't been so drunk I would have been concerned but I just got undressed, got in bed and went to sleep.

When I woke up mom was asleep in the other twin bed. I looked at my phone. It was 10 am. I had the most horrendous hangover. I went to the fridge in the room and got out a bottle of water and drank it. Mom still didn't stir.

After I had showered, I went back into the bedroom and mom was sitting up looking like the cat that had had the cream. Her phone pinged and she picked it up and smirked at a message.

"How was your night?" she said "I don't know where you went. You went off without saying bye. It was lucky Danny was there and I was able to be with him."

She went into the bathroom without waiting for my reply, and I could hear the shower running. When she returned and started getting dressed I asked her if she had had a good time last night with Danny.

"The best time" she said "we had such fun together at the party and then we went back to his place. He has the most beautiful apartment on a higher floor than Keesha's. The views of the city were to die for. I only got back about 6 this morning. It was a night I will never forget."

I felt sick hoping she was going to spare me the details. She didn't say much else until we met Janice for breakfast at McDonalds having decided the hotel breakfast was too expensive. It turned out, Janice had returned to the hotel when I left with Keesha to go downtown. It was mom who had stayed out all night. Mom decided to treat us to an unedited version of her evening with Danny and believe me no detail was spared. I could feel myself blushing! How could a mother talk like that in front of her daughter! I know it had been a few weeks since dad left but she talked like she had been in a sexual desert for years and suddenly came across an oasis. Janice didn't seem embarrassed, instead she seemed to enjoy hearing mom's stories and smiled and laughed along with her.

Mom's phone kept pinging with messages from Danny and he agreed to take us to the airport for our flight which was at 2 pm. He turned up in a BMW looking very casual in ripped jeans and a pure cotton Oxford shirt. I noticed he was wearing an expensive Rolex and a gold ring (not on his wedding finger). He certainly looked like the successful actor. He was also very funny. Much funnier in my opinion than Barry who was supposed to be a comedian. He had us all laughing on the way to the airport.

He dropped us at the "kiss and fly" and promised to keep in touch with mom. I can tell you that mom had turned into a different person to the one who got on the plane to come here yesterday. Mom was glowing and happy. I was pleased for her but hoped she was not getting her hopes up about someone she might never see again.

Once home mom and I went back to our jobs and normality resumed. Mom went back to complaining about the lack of money especially after she had been online and checked the balance on her credit card. Danny had been in touch, and they had been "sexting" to hear her talk. Less said about that the better.

I decided I needed to help out more with money as mom had treated me to the trip to Keesha's party. I handed over some of the tips I had received at the nail salon. "Go and treat yourself mom" I said. She thanked me and took the money…….

Chapter 14

2023 – a New Year

The new year had started bright and sunny in the city. Work was taking place now on the regeneration area and the Institute for the Blind and Visually Impaired had been officially opened. A new store moved into another vacant site. This was a whole foods store that sold vegetables and legumes that were grown on a city farm by the owner. The Mayor was happy with this new store taking a lease in the area and had commissioned a mural for the wall. Work was also started on the playground in Gent Town Park using the federal funding. The Mayor felt he was making an impact on the city.

During the second week of the new term there was another strike at the State University. The unions were seeking a 10% pay rise for all academic staff and longer term contracts for lecturers and instructors that did not have permanent contracts. In addition, for the lowest paid instructors the Unions sought an additional rise to bring them up to an acceptable standard of living. These instructors were often not paid year-round, instead they were only paid when they were actually teaching a class, in other words they were not paid for holidays and any sick time.. Management recommended a 6% pay raise for everyone. Management stated that there was simply not enough money in the budget to meet the Union's demands. The Union refused to compromise and called another strike for the last week in January. In addition, it stated that there was to be a ban on marking student work by its members.

The strike was reported in the *Pinnacle* and discussed on Jerry Leven's radio show. This time the local TV station visited the picket line and interviewed people on the picket line. They also interviewed management. Management talked about a lack of money and budgets. This did not go down well with the public.

Although some people were angry that students were not getting "value for money" due to the strikes, popular opinion was beginning to turn in favour of the striking staff members.

After releasing his memoir "Spare" in January Prince Harry found there was a predictable large amount of coverage in the British Press. The book was a success for the publisher from day one and it was reputed to be selling in large quantities. It was now three years since the duo had left the UK for their new life in the USA. With this book and the documentary there were riding high on worldwide fame.

However, fame came at a cost as in the USA Jimmy Kimmel, a chat show host, made fun of the book on his TV show. He included a skit on the section where the two Princes, William and Harry, allegedly had a fight in the kitchen and Harry broke his necklace and fell into the dog bowl. This was greeted with much laughter from the studio audience and reported in the Press. Another sketch followed where Jimmy Kimmel read from a supposed children's book called "The Prince and the Penis" referring to Harry's frostbitten "todger". This was also greeted with much laughter and people asking if they could buy the book featured on the show.

Maureen Callahan writing in the *Daily Mail* online said

"At times it may be better, as Machiavelli wrote, to be feared than loved. Surely Prince Harry was hoping his memoir would strike fear in the hearts at Buckingham Palace. But what he likely didn't foresee? Becoming a global laughingstock."

Then in February South Park showed an episode on TV called "The Worldwide Privacy Tour". The plot of this episode was a Canadian red headed Prince and his Princess were on a worldwide tour to promote his autobiography "Waagh", yet they demand privacy. The inevitable comparisons ensued with the *Daily Mail* reporting on comments that had been posted on social media. Someone named "Kitty" was quoted as saying "it's bad for Harry and Meghan as this is not a "tribute" but brutal ridicule. (BTW I've been a South Park fan since it began in 1997)"

Could the Duke and Duchess' brand stand up to ridicule, which was different to the many negative reviews and comments they had received previously?.

Jinni - at heart a businesswoman....

In January I was contacted by a TV production company. They asked me if I knew about "Turn back the clock by 15 years" a show they produced? As it turned out I did know about this program. It featured makeovers for people who had "let themselves go". They had basically stopped caring about themselves as they grew older. A resident of the city had been chosen to be in the next show and they were going to give her extensive beauty treatments. They asked if I would be willing to take part and she could come to the salon for her nails to be done. Of course, I agreed! It would be fantastic publicity for the salon. We filmed the lady (Patti Browne) having her nails done on a Sunday when the salon was closed to the public. Although the filming took all morning, the segment shown on TV only lasted a couple of minutes, but I made sure they filmed the entrance to the salon with "The Purple Orchid" logo. I also mentioned the show on my social media advertising "as featured on TV". The salon continued to prosper.

Although there was no visit from Immigration Authorities, I was a little worried that there had been discussions about undocumented workers on the radio. Song continued to work, and I continued to pay in her cash.

I had grown so fond of her, and I could not bear to think of life without her. I would lie in bed, and she would bring me hot tea in the morning and in the evening she would massage my tired shoulders. Having her in my life was like a dream come true.

During January Arpa told me that the orphanage had space for a volunteer and that the volunteer could stay at the orphanage and they would provide all meals. On days off Amara could visit Arpa and stay with her and her family. In the third week in January, Amara told me she would go, but had no funds behind her to support this trip. Her father had left unexpectedly, and her mother now said she had no money. I reassured her that I would give her some spending money to use in Thailand and most important I would pay for her airfare. It was then decided she would go.

The following week Barb came to the salon again at closing time. It was obvious she was furious. I asked her to wait until everyone had left and then I took her into the back room.

"How dare you. How f**king dare you interfere with my family" She shouted at me. I hated the use of profanities.

"Barb" I responded "I know it is upsetting for you that Amara is going to go to Thailand for a few months. But she has lost her way, and this is a good way to help her find a way forward. I am only thinking of the best for her."

"Lost her way?" spluttered Barb "what do you know about it?"

She was shouting now "You have no idea how she behaved at UCLA. It took all of what remained of my savings to bail out her debt."

She continued "Now instead of being there to help me when I need her the most you enable her to go to Thailand and spend time with Somchai's relatives for a few months. She is 21 and these are relatives she has never even met. I think that shows how much they care about us."

Her monologue continued as she began to cry "Have you any idea how hard it is for me with Somchai gone? I can barely make ends meet. How I am going to keep my house and pay all the bills if both my husband and daughter leave within a very short time of each other. Did you think for one minute how this would affect me before you interfered?"

She took a breath here. Her face was red from all the shouting.

"I should have guessed you would interfere. You really are a bitch."

I let her go on – and believe me she said some very nasty things about Somchai, myself and the Thai nation in general. I felt these comments were racist and totally uncalled for. I was determined to keep my cool, however.

"It is what Amara wants" I said "and I am willing to help her so there is no going back now"

By the time she left we were both shaking, she was in tears and I was near to tears. I hoped she wouldn't do anything to prevent Amara going to Thailand. But in reality, I could not imagine what she possibly could do to stop it happening.

A few days later I went into the salon as usual. Song had not been with me the night before, as I had been entertaining my friends at the apartment. When we were all set up and seeing the first customers, I saw that Song had not shown up. Her customer became quite impatient and threatened to leave. I was able to do her nails and give her a discount to stop her complaining.

Song did not show all morning.

Song did not show in the afternoon.

By early afternoon I had moved her customers so that they did not show up without her there.

I became very worried and rang her cell. No answer. I texted her cell. No response.

After work I went to her room. My friend came out of the main house when she saw me arrive.

"She's gone" she said, "she has not paid this week either."

I felt so sick it was hard to talk "Of course, I will make sure the rent is paid. Are you sure she has gone? Have all her things gone?" I asked

We went into her room. It was stripped bare of all her things. She had gone.

When I got home, I messaged her - I texted "You are loved and wanted here. Please come back."

After what seemed like an eternity a message flashed up.

"Lily messaged me to say she had heard that the Immigration Authorities were going to raid the Purple Orchid. She came to get me. I did not want you to get into trouble. We must keep moving as we don't have papers. Don't text again".

Although she was worried about me getting into trouble for employing her, it still seemed that the message was so cold I wondered at first if she had been kidnapped. Yes, I know it sounds mad, but I couldn't believe my darling Song had written that message.

I did try to message again but it wouldn't go through.

My heart was broken. I couldn't believe I would never see her again. I had loved her so much.

I couldn't confide in Somchai as he had warned me about becoming involved.

The next day at 10 a.m. the Purple Orchid was raided by Immigration Authorities. We are an upmarket salon, and this was very difficult for our customers as well as our staff. Of course, Song had gone and there were no undocumented workers working there. They left empty handed. I wondered who had tipped them off?

When I got home, I tried to ring Song to tell her it was okay to come back. But the number was no longer in operation. She had gone to save me I told myself and I didn't know how to find her.

I must be honest and say that I was obsessed with her, and I wanted her back. The first thing I did was to get in touch with her father, the Dean of the College in Guangzhou. I was able to find out his email address from the college website. I wrote in English as I did not know Chinese languages.

I received an email very quickly also written in English.

> "Dear Jinnipha
>
> I was so pleased to hear that Song is alive and well. Song's mother and I have been desperate with worry.
>
> Song arrived in the USA one year ago to study at Highbridge College in Reseda, California. Her grades from

the spring term were poor and she was on academic probation at the college.

During spring 2022 she messaged and wrote regularly. Suddenly in September 2022 the contact ceased. We have heard nothing from her since.

We do not know where she is or what happened to her.

Before this happened, we wanted her to be successful in her own professional career. We talked to her about the importance of good grades and being serious about college. Song preferred popular music and dressing up. Our biggest regret is that we didn't let her do what she wanted. If we had let her have her own way she would be with us here.

How can we begin to search for her in a country the size of the USA? We have put feelers out through the Chinese community, but it is a vast country and I know she has no official papers.

Any help you could give us would be greatly appreciated.

Respectfully signed"

I cried when I read this email. To not even know if your daughter is alive must be torture for these people. They wanted their only child to have a successful professional career and they did not consider if it was also what she wanted. Song was like a child who liked dressing up and beautiful things and people. She was not interested in pouring over books trying to gain knowledge so should could pursue a profession.

If only I had contacted him when she was with me I might have helped the family reconcile. Perhaps I could have talked to the father to explain what it was that Song wanted and liked. She could have stayed working in my salon for as long as she wanted.

I would always carry in my heart the thought of these people who due to my selfish desires I had not contacted. But perhaps now I could make up to them. I was in the USA and could help them look for Song.

These thoughts twirled round and round in my head.

I wondered if I should employ a personal investigator to try to track her down?

I pictured our reunion and her telling me she loved me and that she would never leave me again.

But if I was being honest with myself, would she even want to see me or want to reconcile with her parents?

So here I sit in the back room of the salon sipping some SangSom to take the edge of. In the last few months, I have seen my salon become more and more successful. We are always busy and we have been featured in a TV show. Also, I intend to expand into the new regeneration area. As a business woman I am doing great living in the USA.

But my heart is broken.

Should I follow my heart or my head which was telling me to leave Song well alone?

I really did not know the answer that day.

As these conflicting thoughts swirled round in my head, I took a moment to top my glass up and then I headed out to catch the metro home to make my supper and plan for another day tomorrow where I would face the customers with a smile on my face and make sure that the Purple Orchid continued to give the best manicures and pedicures in the city..

Ellie - makes a surprising discovery....

In the new year my hours had been cut at the State University and I had not been able to find any extra work to make up for this. I was also still working at the small private Catholic college outside the city, but they did not have any extra work for me either. In the second week of term, we went on Strike again. I agreed to be on the picket line, much to the disgust of Kevin.

This time the strike received more attention. The local TV station came to the campus to interview management. They stopped at the picket line and asked if one of us would be interviewed. My colleagues volunteered me to be interviewed. I gave my opinion on the issues that had led to the strike. Salaries were falling behind inflation and part-time lecturers should have more benefits and job security. The interview appeared on our local TV the following evening. Kevin and I were at home watching the news and he was not pleased when he saw that I had spoken up. This time he did not say anything, but his body language spoke volumes.

The next day Libby from Jerry Leven's show rang to ask if I would be interviewed about the strike on the morning commuter show. I agreed to do this, and I also spoke up for the Union on the radio. There were a number of phone-ins from the public, and this time they seemed more positive about the Strike and what the Union were trying to achieve.

I felt I had done the right thing speaking up. Kevin did not own me. I had the right to my own voice and to speak as I wished. "I am sure he will take the extra money if the Union wins in the strike", I said to myself spitefully.

Management would not agree to the Union demands. Another strike was called for the last week in January. In the meantime, we went back to teaching, although there was a ban on marking exams.

One evening we were watching the Jimmy Kimmel show. He did a skit on Prince Harry's book where he (or his writers) had written a poem called "The Prince and the Penis" about Prince Harry suffering frostbite. I have to say, I thought it was very funny. Kevin though found it hilarious. He really laughed long and hard. The studio audience were also laughing.

When he had calmed down Kevin said "See Ellie that is the way to deal with a Prince who has got out of hand. From what I have heard on the news there are a lot of scandalous revelations about his family in his book "Spare". Things that would be best kept private. Yes, he is making a lot of money selling his family down the river and he seems a very angry person. The British are all steamed up and angry about him. Jimmy Kimmel is treating the situation with humour. It is very hard to be taken seriously when you are being sent up. If only you could have listened to Jimmy Kimmel before you put your rantings onto YouTube"

"You are a pompous, arrogant pig" I shouted at him "how dare you patronise me? Who do you think you are?"

"Come on Ellie" he said "stop being so sensitive. What is wrong with you? I feel I can't talk to you anymore. You don't seem to be able to see the other side of any situation You don't listen and are so emotional."

"Shut up! Shut up!" I screamed. I ran upstairs and looked myself in the bathroom.

I just wanted to get away from him. But where would I go? I was in a foreign country and earned next to nothing. I couldn't even afford to pay for a motel room. I could not go back to England as I was distant from what family I had.

There was only one place I could go. I went to the bedroom and rang Kara who had become a friend from my visits to the nail salon. I asked if I could go over to her home.

She seemed pleased to hear from me and said it was fine.

I got in the car and drove over to Kara's apartment. When I got there her two girls were in bed and she was in the living room with a glass of wine waiting for me. Kara's husband had left her for a much younger woman. She was not a big fan of marriage.

Her apartment was only small, but it felt so warm and friendly. I loved her decorating style. We sat chatting and drinking wine until about 2 am. Kara made up the pull-out sofa bed for me in the living room and I slept there that night. .

As I was getting ready for bed, Kevin sent me a text "Come home Ellie" it said "Stop being so silly. You know I love you".

I lay awake for most of the night. There was something else that I had not told either Kevin or Kara. This related to the sickness I had felt for the last couple of weeks. My breasts were bigger than ever. In fact, I would describe them as ginormous. Plus, and very important I was late. This was very unusual for me, but I had not wanted to take a test. I thought if I ignored it, it would go away. But it was not going away. Kevin and I both wanted children, but we had been putting this off until our financial position got better. How on earth were we going to afford a baby? We were barely getting by as it was.

I knew that I had to go and take a pregnancy test tomorrow and then I would know for sure.

I went to the pharmacy on the way to the University. I don't know how I got through my classes that day. I finally plucked up courage to take the test and it came back positive.

I knew that I had to go home and face Kevin. I rang Kara and thanked her for putting me up last night, but I had to go home and try to talk to Kevin.

I let myself into the house. It was quiet and tidy. Kevin had not returned from work. I sat alternatively panicking and feeling excited on the sofa. I was going to be someone's mom. This was really going to alter everything.

At 7 pm I heard Kevin's key in the lock. He walked in looking pale and tired.

"Why did you have to go off like that Ellie?" he asked "you should be able to take a little bit of criticism".

"Kevin" I stood up "please shut up for once. I have something I need to tell you..."

And then I told him my news...........

Janine - living the good life.....

Gene and I were enjoying our new home. We had had a housewarming party for our friends, and we also decided to invite Amy and Granny around and I would cook them a healthy meal. Everyone enjoyed it and we talked about eating healthily and exercising.

The pastor at Amy and Granny's church was impressed by how their mobility had increased and had asked them to give a talk at The Church Women's Club. They had given this talk but had met with a very divided audience. Some women were impressed with what they were doing and asked for tips. A couple of middle-aged women even said they would join us at the "Couch to 5k".

However, Amy and Granny were surprised by the number of people who were very anti to their talk.

"We only have one life, and the Good Lord wants us to enjoy our time on this earth" one woman had said "why should we have to deny ourselves food we enjoy? I also like a few drinks each evening. I don't want to live to be old if it means being miserable!"

Another woman had chimed in "My granny lived until she was 100 and she smoked 60 cigarettes a day and drank whiskey every night! She also had a very "poor" diet in your eyes which consisted of meat and potatoes".

Someone else said "there is no proof all this exercise and healthy eating works. I feel it is a lot of stress on old bones jogging and running at your age. Also, I like traditional food, meat and potatoes and pumpkin pie. I can't believe you are saying this is not good for me. Why deny yourself what you like?"

Amy and granny were frustrated that they were not able to handle the people better who were against exercise and eating healthily. They were not used to speaking up in public and being questioned.

After they had left Gene said he felt the exercise and healthy eating was really working out well for them. They just needed to develop a bit more confidence dealing with people who challenged their views. He said that he would spend some time with them to help them be confident in speaking up in public. He had to make speeches as part of his job. If you are speaking persuasively, he said you must understand your audience and try to meet their needs. If the audience has never run or jogged and likes hearty food then you can encourage them to manage their expectations so that they can feel better and still eat well. If you threaten to take everything they love away from them immediately then you won't have their compliance. It should be a gradual thing. Start with small steps. Perhaps when going shopping they could consider getting off the metro one stop early and walking, for example. Then move it up to two stops and then eventually walk to the shops. The same with food, perhaps have less potatoes and more green vegetables to start. And so on. It seemed to make sense to me as this is what we were doing with the "Couch to 5k" gradually building up the amount of time we spent running.

I had agreed to another mural commission – this time on the side of a building that was to be opened as a whole foods shop in the regeneration area. This would sell healthy products that had been grown at a City Farm. I arranged to go and meet the owner of the farm, Gary Brinker. He recommended that I visit the farm to get a better understanding of what he was trying to achieve.

The farm was at the far end of the northern suburbs where the city was giving way to open countryside. Gary showed me around explaining his ethos. "I am into sustainable farming. I don't use chemical-based pesticides or fertilisers."

The farm was only small and divided into distinct areas where he grew vegetables, fruits, herbs and flowers.

Gary told me that a local charity for disadvantaged youths volunteered at the farm. Young people came to help. They learned how crops are grown and how to cultivate crops and pick them for a harvest. Once a month they had a cooking lesson.

The food that was harvested was at present sold on a stall at the side of the road. However, the shop in the regeneration area would be a big expansion project for the farm.

He said that he wanted to open a café in the shop selling healthy snacks and drinks.

We discussed the mural. I had already begun to picture it in my mind. I pictured the bright colours of the vegetables and fruits that Gary was growing. I also pictured young people bending over and tending the crops.

Gary felt it would be a good idea to show the young people tending the crops. He recommended visiting again when they were there so I could see them at work on the farm.

I went away with lots of ideas in my head and looking forward to sketching them out.

So as January rolled over into February, I was very busy with designing the new mural and enjoying my new home. I was feeling fitter and much healthier with the running and healthy eating and becoming more optimistic that we could take part in the 5k in March. I knew I had so many blessings, but I prayed for one more the gift of a child and who knew what the spring would bring...

A spicy healthy recipe

This dish give you all the flavour of the famous dish Singapore chili crab, but in a vegetarian version, substituting tofu for the crab meat means that the bland tofu can soak up the spicy flavour of the sauce.

Ingredients:

1 tbs cornstarch whisked with 2 tablespoons of water.
2 tbs peanut oil
4 birds eye chilis. (Remove the seeds and inner veins from the chilis for a slightly milder effect.)
2 tbs grated peeled ginger
4 garlic cloves, minced finely
2 green onions, finely chopped
2tbs tomato paste
¼ tsp white pepper
1tbs demerara sugar
300 ml vegetable stock
200 grammes of firm plain tofu – cubed
100 ml chili & garlic sauce

Speed is of the essence with this dish, as the tofu must not break down much, so it is important to have all ingredients ready before cooking begins.

Warm the oil to a medium heat in a wide frying pan or wok and add the ginger, garlic chilis and most of the whites of the spring onion. Stir fry very briefly (about 30seconds) to warm the ingredients and create a lovely aroma. Do not allow the ingredients to burn.

Add the tomato paste, sugar and white pepper and stir for 2 to 3 minutes to combine and to form a paste.

Next add the vegetable stock and bring to a simmer. This will make the mixture much looser so that the tofu can soak up the flavours.

When the stock mixture is simmering, add the cubed tofu and stir, simmering for 5 minutes until the tofu is warmed through.

Finally, add the cornstarch water mixture, stir and see the mixture thicken again, stirring occasionally. After 3 or 4 minutes it will be ready to serve in bowls, topped with a scatter of the remaining green spring onion leaves.

Amara – finding her roots.....

I finally plucked up courage to tell mom about the opportunity to live in Thailand for a few months and volunteer at an orphanage.

"Oh right" she said "and how are we going to afford that? We can hardly afford to live day to day with your father doing a runner."

After she said that she stopped and stared at me as suddenly it hit her.

"OMG" she said "this has to be either your father or Jinni. And given what I have heard about your father's financial situation I doubt it is him. It's Jinni, isn't it? She is going to pay for you to fly out to Thailand and your living expenses, correct?"

I told mom that Jinni was going to pay my airfare. Although I was volunteering at the orphanage and didn't get paid in cash, I could stay there for free, and they would provide meals. On days off my Thai relatives would visit me and take me on days out. I would not need much money.

"So, she is not content with aiding and abetting your father to leave" mom said, "now she wants you to leave as well."

She then broke down in tears. Her shoulders heaved in great big sobs.

I was at a loss what to do. I wasn't used to seeing mom act vulnerable.

Cautiously I moved over to her and put my arms around her.

"Mom, you know I love you and would never leave you" I said "this is just for 2 or 3 months and then I will be home."

We sat cuddling for a few moments and I felt like I might have reached her.

However, I then found out through the grapevine that the following day she went to the salon and yelled at Auntie Jinni.

I was determined to go to Thailand, and I applied to the orphanage and for a visa online. The orphanage were delighted to have me volunteer there for 3 months starting in February. I make arrangements so that I could fly out there early in February.

Meanwhile I told dad that I had made my mind up and I was going to go. He seemed happy for me and promised to give me some "spending money".

Meanwhile filming on the soap opera "Grangemouth" was taking a break. The cast were waiting to see if it would be renewed for a second series. Danny had messaged mom and had agreed with her that he would come and visit us while he was "resting". Although it would have been quicker to fly he decided to drive to our home. It was a long drive but this way he could bring clothes and personal items for an extended stay.

One day there was just mom and me and the next day he was suddenly there in our home. He was a larger-than-life character, I have to say. He was very funny, but loud. It was like when he arrived, he took over dominating the conversations and acting as if it was his home and he owned it. I would get back from work at the nail salon, and he would be there with a glass in his hand, holding forth to mom. They would be cooking together, which as you can imagine, was a sight to behold as mom can't cook. He was very patient with her, and they cooked simple dishes. We would eat spaghetti Bolognese or meatloaf. Often though he would say "Lets order takeout" and he would order us food from UberEats. We had some good meals when he paid, I must say. He would spend a fortune on Chinese food. He couldn't use chop sticks though and mom would tease him, and we would all laugh at his efforts.

I hoped he was going to give her some money to contribute towards his stay in addition to the UberEats, but mom seemed happy in any event and had put her money worries on the back burner since he turned up. I got to checking Deadline every day to see if the soap had been renewed. I wondered what would happen if it was not renewed and Danny stayed with us on a long-term basis. He was definitely a presence in our home.

He would lounge around in the evening watching TV and giving us a commentary on the movies and shows. This was always really funny and light hearted. One night we were watching the Jimmy Kimmel show and Jimmy read out a poem called "The Prince and the Penis". This was a skit on Prince Harry's book Spare so far as I could work out where Prince Harry said he had frost bite on his "todger" as he called it. It was funny and mom and I laughed, but Danny thought it was hilarious. Danny and mom were exchanging looks and laughing. I felt embarrassed as if I should not have been in the room with them, although it was just knowing looks and laughter.

I guess thinking of the Jimmy Kimmel sketch reminds of the other thing Danny did that was really strange. He liked to skinny dip in our pool even though it was January. In winter I do not go in the pool as I believe it is too cold, but Danny said the cold is good for your health and it can stimulate release of endorphins. I would wake up, look out my window, and see his bare ass swimming up and down the pool. He would walk out of the house clad in just a towel which he would drop as he walked to get into the pool. I don't know if he knew I was at the window. But it seemed, he didn't mind who saw him without clothes on. He would drop the towel and turn to face the house. Of course, this was very disrespectful. There was always the chance that I was looking and if he knew that I was there he should not be naked in front of his host and partner's daughter. I know I should have looked away but looking back I wonder if he got pleasure knowing or fantasising that I saw him? He was very well endowed. Even outside on a relatively cold January morning. Mom was not making the stories up about her sex life with him, even though it was entirely inappropriate that she had shared them with me. I suppose it was no wonder she seemed so happy. But it was also very uncomfortable for me being there and being with someone who behaved like he did. I should have been grossed out and I should have turned away, but to be honest, I was curiously mesmerised by seeing him. It felt like I was seeing something secret and illicit, and on the days that he did this I would duck behind the drapes and watch him. Then I would get dressed and turn up at the nail salon feeling strangely aroused. Why on earth would I feel like that about my mother's partner? He was really old, even older than my dad. He had a good body though, which I think he kept in shape by running and lifting weights at the gym in Vinings Village. Why I looked or cared was mad. The whole thing was ridiculous.

To be honest I was relieved I was getting away for a few months. I felt more mixed up than ever having Danny living with us. However, sometimes you never know how lucky you are, and Auntie Jinni's idea of volunteering at the orphanage in Thailand was the best ever. I am so lucky to have her as my Auntie.

On the day I was due to leave mom had taken some time off work to drive me to the airport. I was going to fly to Atlanta and change there for Bangkok. I had two big cases and a backpack. At the airport we both ended up in tears and hugging each other.

"Don't you dare turn your phone off or not write to me regularly" mom said.

"I promise I will message as soon as I arrive" I said

The flight to Atlanta was very short but when I got on the long haul to Bangkok I was just settling in when, you won't believe this, I noticed a really cute guy sitting across the aisle. It turned out that he was going to Bangkok for an extended holiday as he had just broken up with his girlfriend.

So here I am on a long haul flight with a drink of wine in my hand chatting to a cute guy and suddenly the future seems very bright indeed.

Chapter 15

Epilogue – spring comes to the City

So, our story ends at the beginning of February 2023. The last six months had been very eventful in the city and for the four friends.

The new Mayor had introduced his strategy to the city. He had begun to rejuvenate the rundown district to the north of downtown and was applying for federal funding for his various initiatives. His Charity Ball had been a huge success and the idea of Street Art had been introduced with a mural unveiled on the new Institute for the Blind and Visually Impaired and more murals planned.

Under the new Mayor many people felt the city was a good place to live. There was full employment and real estate prices boomed.

It was a good time to have a business in the city, and the Purple Orchid had become even more popular and financially lucrative.

There were still some complaints about violence and recently about illegal immigrants but in the main it was a great time to live in the city.

Although Jinni had seen her salon, The Purple Orchid, become very popular and financially lucrative, she had threatened this success by employing Song, an undocumented alien. Not just employing Song but falling in love with her and Jinni's heart was broken when Song left without leaving a forwarding address. Additionally, the visit by Immigration Authorities had caused gossip about the salon which could potentially affect future profits.

Jinni had also interfered in the life of her niece, Amara, who was working as a manicurist at the Purple Orchid. Amara had dropped out of university in the spring of 2022 and seemed to have lost her way. Jinni helped Amara find volunteer work at an orphanage in Bangkok and Amara left in February 2023 to find her roots and plan for her future life.

Ellie, the Englishwoman who had been finding her voice in the fall, speaking up in meetings, on the radio and on YouTube had just found out she was expecting a baby. How would her husband Kevin react when they were barely making ends meet as it was?

Janine was gaining some success with her artwork – having just received a second commission from the Mayor for a mural in the regeneration area. She was also running with her granny and Amy and eating healthily. Her husband had just been made a partner in a CPA firm and they had bought a beautiful home. She had so many blessings and she felt a child would be the icing on the cake.

The last few months had also been eventful for the Duke and Duchess of Sussex. Over this period, they had been in the mainstream media almost continually. Whether reporting on the Duchess podcast or their docuseries for Netflix or the Duke's memoir "Spare" the media remained fascinated by the duo. And so, they continued to be divisive and much talked and gossiped about. However, also over these months we can see a difference in how they were talked about. The British media continued to report on them provoking divisive comments some of which were angry. By February 2023 American celebrities and media seemed to be having some fun with them provoking laughter, the world over. This was very different, and it is interesting to see how this would play out in the future. It could be that by provoking laughter in others the duo would become even more popular. As Maya Angelou said "At the end of the day people won't remember what you said or did, they will remember how you made them feel." If you made them feel happy by making them laugh what better remembrance is there?

Although it is now time to finish our story, perhaps one day we will return to the city and after parking in the underground garage stroll along the Walks until we come to the doorway surrounded by bougainvillea that takes us into the Purple Orchid. Once inside we can breathe in the perfume from the exotic flowers and listen and take part in the chatter and gossip ……

Printed in Great Britain
by Amazon

44433965R00126